ALSO BY
FREDERICK BARTHELME

Moon Deluxe

Second Marriage

Frederick Barthelme

SIMON AND
SCHUSTER
NEW YORK

Copyright © 1984 by Frederick Barthelme
All rights reserved
including the right of reproduction
in whole or in part in any form
Published by Simon and Schuster
A Division of Simon & Schuster, Inc.
Simon & Schuster Building
Rockefeller Center
1230 Avenue of the Americas
New York, New York 10020
SIMON AND SCHUSTER and colophon are registered trademarks of
Simon & Schuster, Inc.
Designed by Irving Perkins
Manufactured in the United States of America
1   3   5   7   9   10   8   6   4   2
Library of Congress Cataloging in Publication Data
Barthelme, Frederick, date.
Second Marriage.
I. Title.
PS3552.A763S4   1984   813'.54   84-10572
ISBN: 0-671-47441-3
Portions of this book first appeared
in different form in The New Yorker.

For Veronica

"Mortar didn't bite," Jerry said, tapping the loose brick. "He's gonna get epoxied in there tomorrow."

"I hate that stuff," Grace said. "Jerry uses it on everything."

I stubbed my toe against a couple more bricks so he would know that I knew the others were O.K.

"Where do you folks live now?" Jerry asked. He stood up and slapped his hands against each other to get the dust off. "You looking for an investment or what?"

"We have an apartment," Theo said. "We've had this apartment for ninety years and I've got to get out of it before I bust wide open."

"An apartment," Grace said. "That's easy, I'll bet."

"Yep," I said. I nodded at her.

"That's why he likes it," Theo said. "His father made him do yard work until he was twenty."

"I hated yard work," Jerry said. "But you get used to it after a while. Sometimes it's even fun."

"I like to water," I said.

"Know what you mean," he said.

"You don't know what he means, Jerry," Grace said. "How could you know what he means? You never water."

"That's not the point."

"Well if that's not the point I don't know what is," she said. Grace was tiny and immaculate. Jerry was like the fat kid from high school. His pants looked as if they were made out of olive loaf.

They walked us in circles through the house and talked materials, age, renovations. "When he built the fireplace he was really supposed to be building a bathroom off here," Grace said. We were in the master bedroom and she was pointing at a wall with a small window in it. "This is the back porch out here." She tapped the window glass. "We planned to drop a tub right out here and use the other one for guests, but he wanted the fireplace."

"You wanted it, too, Kitten."

She smoothed her blouse. "I didn't want it more than

the tub, Jerry. Remember? You asked me which one I wanted more and I was still thinking about it when you started ripping out the big wall."

In the kitchen Grace told us how much she disliked the brown appliances. "We got them from Jerry's mother," she said. "One of the great things about moving to Arkansas is that I get to buy a new stove and refrigerator." They were selling because she'd gotten a job in the history department at a university in Little Rock.

When the tour was done Theo and I went out to the porch to do our talking and they sat side by side on the cream sofa that faced the fireplace. From the porch I watched the backs of their heads as they waited.

"I know I want it," Theo said.

"Well, why don't we think about it," I said. "I feel silly buying a place from kids. And we're doing fine in the apartment."

"You are," she said.

We talked a few minutes, then got up and took a walk down the street, talking more. We walked through the neighborhood, on the sidewalks, which were leaf-strewn and nicely cracked. Theo looked pretty walking in the leaves, at ease and lovely. She picked up a twig and carried that with her. Nobody else was around. We were gone twenty minutes, and when we got back to the house Theo said she wanted it and she was buying it.

"I see," I said.

"Yes," she said.

We went in and she told Jerry and Grace. Jerry shook my hand and said it was a deal. Grace thought we ought to have champagne to celebrate. She brought out Jerry's French horn and he played "Greensleeves," or something that sounded like it, while she looked on admiringly.

When we were in bed at the apartment that night Theo said, "I guess we can get married now."

I had asked her to marry me two years earlier, but she hadn't wanted to. She said we were doing fine living to-

gether. She said we were too old. She said it was risky, and
that we could do it if I insisted, but she thought it was a
bad idea.

So we didn't get married until the day after we closed
the house deal.

Grace had a friend who was an Episcopal priest. He came
over and married us on the front lawn, with Jerry and Grace
bearing witness, and Rachel waiting patiently for us to get
it over with. Jerry played the Wedding March on his horn
and passersby slowed their Buicks and Oldsmobiles to watch
the ceremony. The priest wanted to make an occasion of
it, so he sat all of us down in folding chairs and gave us a
talk. I looked up and down the street, catching glimpses of
our new neighbors framed in their windows.

The bank officer who made the house loan was at the
wedding. He said he thought we'd be very happy together.
He said the marriage made him feel a lot better.

A stiff-looking guy in orange shorts came out of the house
across the street and stood on his porch with a glass in one
hand and the other hand tucked inside the sagging elastic
of his waistband. When the priest was done, and Jerry had
finished some kind of good-luck tune, the guy across the
street yelled, "You got a permit?" He waited a minute while
we all looked at him, then turned and went back into his
house, locking the door elaborately once he was inside.

"Mr. Armstrong," Grace said. "He lives there with his
mother. I think they're moving, though."

A couple of weeks later I was in the yard brushing red paint
on a wooden chair we'd bought at Woolco. Theo was inside,
watching me through the window. Duncan Brown, the first
neighbor we actually met when we moved in, was in his
driveway washing his wire-haired terrier, Jupiter, and Duncan too was watching me paint. He was younger than we
were. All our neighbors, except perhaps Mr. Armstrong and

the people who lived in the tile two-story on the corner, seemed like kids. This bothered me. Even Theo was six years younger than me. I mentioned this to her and she said, "Oh, don't be silly."

I stopped painting for a minute and watched Theo. She had one of Rachel's toy helicopters in her hand and she was pretending to crash it into the den window. Then she quit that and sat there spinning the toy blades.

Duncan Brown leaped over the bushes that separated our yard from his. "What do you want to paint that chair for, Henry?" he said, smacking his hands at his khaki pants.

I waved my brush, depositing a row of red paint drops on the grass. Duncan already thought of us as old friends. In two weeks the Browns were the only neighbors we had spent any time with, although some woman who lived two houses down had sent her maid over with a beef pie the day we moved, and Theo kept saying we ought to have the woman to dinner. Duncan was a lawyer of some kind and his wife, Cindy, was a non-practicing architect. They were both about thirty. Their house was cobalt blue with navy-blue trim. She had gone to school in San Francisco and she said everybody out there painted houses interesting colors. "People aren't afraid of color on the Coast the way they are here," she said when we met. I told her I liked lavender a lot. Theo sighed at me.

The chair I was painting was one Duncan had broken the week before. He tipped over in it after dinner while showing us a peculiar mark he'd found on his ankle. Now he looked at the chair with disdain. "No reason you should hang on to a chair like that," he said.

"Theo wants it in Rachel's room," I said, waving the brush again, dry this time. That wasn't true. I was doing it for Rachel because she had always wanted a red chair.

Her father was a guitar player named Cale. He had met Theo at an office party when she worked downtown, and they had used the roof for lovemaking. Six months later I met Theo at a party. After everyone had played pat-the-baby and who's-the-father, I handed Theo her coat and walked her out the front door, without a word. It was a wonderful move. I was especially grateful for her cooperation.

Courtship followed. A long, periodic courtship. That's when I learned about Cale, about the roof, and about the other things you learn when you see someone constantly. Two years later, on the baby's second birthday, I moved in. I tried to get on as adjunct faculty at the university, but they didn't need me, so I got a job doing paste-up for an ad agency.

Theo quit her night job with campus security after a rapist football star nearly killed her when she caught him crawling out the window of an off-campus housing unit. She talked her way into a job with the Conferences and Workshops section of the university, a PR function which had her traveling in the region, trying to sell small corporations on the idea of using university facilities for annual meetings. We had enough money to move into a better place at The Gardens, a two-hundred-unit apartment-condominium development on the west side of town. That place burned a year and a half later, so we stretched things a little and leased an apartment at Lakefront, an expensive development bordering a saltwater lake that was fed, through a complex of man-made canals, by the Gulf of Mexico. Then came the house.

Duncan Brown tiptoed in a circle, looking at the chair. "How about them Birds?" he said, skirting the painted grass.

"What Birds?"

Duncan twirled his eyes and sat down with his back against a pole. "I forgot that you hate sports. Or maybe I didn't forget, maybe I was making fun of myself. Self-effacing, you know?"

"Oh. *Those* Birds." I slapped a brushload of paint on the

chair seat. "Just a slump. Don't worry about it."

Baseball was important to Duncan. He thought it a re-
markable human achievement. I wasn't so fond of it, though
I could watch a few innings on television now and then.
"I've only got a minute." he said. "There was this guy,
an umpire in the big leagues. He was old, made a lot of
bad calls. It was obvious. Season after season they couldn't
get rid of him. He had a stroke in the middle of a game.
The other umpires and the players gathered around. These
were middle-age men, mostly, with pimpled rookies scattered in, toward the back. All shuffling their feet, digging
cleats into the turf, looking grave. In the ambulance, this
umpire slipped his mask into place, crooked a finger at the
attendant. 'Boy,' he said. 'Remember this: I never called
one wrong in my heart.'"

Duncan stared at me. When I nodded, he said, "That's
all." He looked around the yard as if he expected to find
something behind a tree or hidden in the bushes. "Where's
Theo?"

"Inside. There's a primate-psychology thing on TV."

"The big gorilla," he said, nodding. "Suddenly they want
savvy marketing advice. I knew it was coming." He pointed
toward the den. "Nevertheless, that looks like her in the
window there, struggling with a helicopter. Were you, perhaps, waving a red herring?"

"Wasn't red," I said.

I invited him for a sandwich, but he didn't want to stay.
After lunch, Rachel said, "I have something to tell you."
She was grinning and winking wildly.

"What's wrong with your face?"

"Come here." She stamped her foot and wiggled a forefinger at me, demanding that I follow her into the kitchen.
I did as she asked and she put her arm around my neck,
squeezing gently. "I played doctor yesterday," she said.
"Really. With Richie Farmer. I guess it's late for me to do
that, huh?"

I made a horror-movie scared-out-of-my-wits look. "How'd

you like it?" It was my best guess at a correct response.

She said, "Boy, I don't ever want to do that again. It was stupid. He's funny-looking."

"Who's funny-looking?" Theo said. She was still at the dinner table, folding napkins.

"Nobody," Rachel said.

"You are," I said. "She thinks you got a dumb haircut."

"I did not say that." Rachel punched a thumb into my side. "I didn't say that, Mom."

"You think it's dumb?" Theo said, poking at her new short hair with her fingers, fluffing the hair and looking at herself in the dark window. "I think it makes me look kind of mysterious."

"Like a dyke," Rachel said. "Yeah."

I knuckled her head. "Miss Rachel is exhibiting inappropriate behaviors," I said. "Miss Rachel's going to have Tide for dessert if she doesn't straighten out."

"I'm sorry," Rachel said, hanging her head. "Lesbian."

"These young people today," Theo said. She looked at me and pointed to Rachel. "She's only forty and here she is familiar with the concept of homosexuality—what do you make of that?"

"I think we'd better get her cleaned up pretty quick," I said.

"I want a computer for my birthday," Rachel said.

———— • ————

F OR THE first few weeks we had almost no furniture in the house. We hadn't had much at the apartment, so we were used to it, but Duncan Brown kept popping in and asking where the chairs were, so Theo started buying design magazines.

"We're going to do this right," she told me.

I drew a scaled floor plan of the house and we cut out squares of black paper to represent pieces of furniture and moved those around on the drawing. Unfortunately, the furniture Theo liked in the magazines was much more expensive than we could afford, so we began to lose interest in the project. We decided to leave things bare until we could buy the kind of furniture we wanted.

Then Theo found a picture of a leather-covered dining chair she loved and decided we should have one wonderful thing in the house, so she called New York to see how much the chair was. When she came back into the living room, where we'd been playing with the floor plan and the paper cutouts, she said, "They want eighteen hundred and seventy dollars for this." She rattled the magazine that had the photograph of the chair in it. "I told the guy it was just a dining chair and then he got snooty. How much are chairs, usually?"

"Fifty dollars," I said.

"You just sit in them," Rachel said. "You can't even see them when you're in them."

"Good point," I said.

"Who can buy this chair?" Theo said. "Frigging Aga Khan can't afford this chair in numbers sufficient to seat his immediate family."

15

"Who?" Rachel said.

"Somebody my mother always talked about," Theo said. She dumped the magazine on the table and then stood looking at the room. "I'm never, in my whole life, until the day I die, never am I going to own this chair. Isn't that crazy?"

"That's semi-crazy, Mom," Rachel said. She got off her knees and gave Theo a hug. "I'm sorry."

"I almost bought the damn thing just to show the creep I could," Theo said. "I should've told him to send me a dozen."

"You're getting hostile, Mom." Rachel spun away from Theo and put on a thoughtful expression, rubbing her jaw. "If I was them I'd just give you one, just for liking it so much."

I put my arm around Rachel. "We'd better keep your mother away from the death ray for the time being."

"I want some pie," Theo said. "Is there any of that pie left in the refrigerator?"

"I ate it," Rachel said. "I had a pie attack this morning."

"What are daughters for?" Theo said. She went into the bedroom and came out a minute later with her purse in one hand and her espadrilles in the other. "I'm going to get a pie. I'm not going to get anything else, however, so don't ask."

"What kind of pie?" Rachel said. "Are you going to Pie Country or what?"

"Pie Country," she said. "Yes."

"Maybe we ought to go with her," Rachel said to me. "She looks distraught. Besides, I want an éclair and some peanut-butter ice cream and a box of Choco-Mints."

Theo balanced herself against the doorframe and stepped into the shoes. "I told you you can't have Choco-Mints anymore, Rachel. Dr. Bob says they eat you more than you eat them."

"Dr. Bob's a real great guy, for a Nazi," Rachel said. "He

should be a dog dentist instead of a real dentist." She tugged on my shirtsleeve. "You remember what he told me? He said I should eat the occasional dog biscuit to keep the scum under control. Can you believe that?"

"He was kidding, Rachel," Theo said. She jerked her head toward the kitchen and the back door. "Let's go if we're going."

"He should do his jokes at the pound," Rachel said.

My first wife, Clare, was at Pie Country. I didn't see much of Clare, but Theo saw her often. Clare had come back to town and gotten a job at the university. They had become friends, though Theo never brought Clare home. When they got together they met at a restaurant, or at the spa where Clare was a member, or at the track. Clare led us across the restaurant to her table so she could introduce her boyfriend, Joel, who was a smallish guy with more muscles than he really needed. He was wearing a light-blue V-neck sweater and aviator glasses.

Theo told Clare about the house, and I said something to Joel about the Birds.

"What Birds?" he said.

"That's baseball for you," Rachel said.

He smiled at her, a short, plastered-on smile that she didn't seem to notice but that I found particularly unpleasant. "You're in advertising, is that right?"

"In and out," I said.

"He's an out-of-work professor," Rachel said. She looped her arm through mine as if to protect me as we stood by the table and waited for Theo.

"Have you tried the Baptist College? I hear they've got a hell of a turnover out there. And lots of money."

I nodded. "I keep the resumés going around. But for the moment it's advertising."

"Sure," he said. "Something's gonna break for you here

pretty quick." He picked up his fork and fiddled with the banana pie on his plate.

"Hey, Hank," Rachel said, pulling me toward the rear of the restaurant. "C'mon. Hurry. She just cleaned up the big round booth back here."

I held off her charge long enough for a quick handshake with Joel. "Pleased to meet you," I said. Then I tapped Theo on the back, pointed to the booth with the round table, and let Rachel drag me away. When we were safely out of the others' hearing, I said, "I guess you thought I couldn't handle it?"

"You were looking pretty rocky there for a minute," she said. She slid into the booth, bouncing to test the seat cushion. "Besides, we'd have lost the booth. This is the best booth in the place."

A skinny waitress dropped two wedge-shape plastic menus on the outside edge of the table and said, "Help yall?" She was chewing gum. She had on a pink waffle-textured uniform. Her apron was brown and it had a lot of discouraging spots on it.

"We need three," I said, pointing to the menus. "Somebody coming."

The waitress looked over her shoulder. "Somebody coming?" she said, as if she suspected funny business. "That woman there?"

"That's our mom," Rachel said. Then she scratched her face by drumming her fingers on her cheekbone—a new habit.

The waitress wasn't pleased, but left the table to get another menu from the triangular bin alongside the cash register. Rachel, meanwhile, pushed herself up and did a belly flop on the table reaching for the two menus we already had.

I shoved them a little to put them within her range. "It was the sweater," I said. "I could've handled the tan, even the black watch, but the sweater was too much."

"What about the shades?"

"I could go either way on the shades," I said.

She was bent over the menu, running her finger down the list of pies. I looked at my menu. The list was numbered. There were forty kinds of pies on the list, but many seemed to be variations of each other. Pineapple Upside Down Pie and Pineapple Meringue and Pineapple Crunch Pie Supreme all caught my eye.

Rachel was hard at work on the menu, her finger on pie thirty, Pumpkin Cinnamon Escape. "I wish you were my father," she said.

"What do you think I am?" I reached to brush her hair, but she bumped my hand away.

"I saw this show about people going all over trying to find their real parents," she said. "I guess I'm going to have to do that someday."

"You've got a while yet." I fanned my menu at a fly that buzzed over my head. I watched the fly jag in the rush of air, then circle for a second pass. Instead of coming back it landed above me and started walking down the wall. I waved my menu again.

"Something the matter, sir?" It was the waitress, back with the third menu.

"I was just taking a look at your paneling," I said.

"An architect," Rachel said, taking the menu from the woman. "What happened to the Blueberry Hill?"

"I don't know," the waitress said. She leaned over my shoulder and sighted down my list of pies. "I don't see it here at all. Used to be right on there around ten, didn't it?"

The girl was wearing a scent I recognized, one I'd smelled before, but not one of the easy ones. "That's a nice perfume," I said.

"It's Daydreams," she said. "I used to wear Nuance all the time, but everybody's doing that now, so I switched."

"No Blueberry Hill, huh?" Rachel said.

The waitress shook her head. "I guess it didn't go over. If it went over you bet Art would've kept it on." She looked up the aisle at Theo, who was half in and half out of Clare's booth.

"I'll have coffee and a piece of chocolate—have you got a plain chocolate pie?"

"Sure," the girl said. She hit the eraser of her pencil on Double-Boiled Chocolate Rollover on my menu.

"Fine," I said. "Rachel?"

"I want two scoops of peanut-butter ice cream, a Coke, and a piece of this number twenty-seven."

"Twenty-seven?" the waitress said, bending over me again to look at my menu.

"Pirate Marble Pecan," Rachel said. "Whatever that is."

"Right," the waitress said. "You want me to get your wife on my way back?" She pointed the pencil over her shoulder toward Theo.

"Just bring an extra coffee," I said.

"She doesn't like coffee anymore," Rachel said. "Why doesn't she come sit down like the rest of us? She always does this."

"She doesn't get out much," I said, waving at the waitress. "Coffee's fine."

"I don't know why I ordered that pecan thing," Rachel said, looking at me with her head resting on one finger. "I hate pecans, don't I? Did you really think that waitress smelled good? I thought she stunk."

"She was O.K.," I said.

Rachel looked around Pie Country, shaking her head. "I saw this thing on television. I think that's why I said that about you being my real father. I mean, you are my father, really. Right? Oh, this is stupid. Forget it. You got any quarters? I want to play a game."

"They don't have games here," I said. "I don't have any quarters anyway."

"I want a dirt bike. Can I have a dirt bike? I'll be real careful."

"I thought you wanted a computer."

"I do, but I want a dirt bike too. Julio Epstein has a dirt bike and a computer."

"Who's Julio Epstein?"

"Oh, you know. You met his mother at that stupid Halloween party. She was dressed up like a windmill or something."

I shook my head and sat back so our waitress could slide the coffee, Coke, pie, and ice cream onto our table. "Don't remember," I said.

There was a stir down the aisle when Theo, Clare, and Clare's boyfriend all stood up at once. Theo shrieked and jumped back and then something glass hit the floor. Our waitress said, "Bingo."

"Looking good," Rachel said. "Way to hop, Mom."

I gave Rachel a look and she dug into the ice cream.

"I'm not cleaning it up this time," our waitress said to me. "I don't care if Jennie has wooden legs, I'm not cleaning it up for her."

A short red-haired girl came out from behind the counter carrying a rag the size of a beach towel.

"I'll bet she doesn't really have wooden legs," Rachel said. There was a drip of brown ice cream on her lip.

"Wipe your mouth. Here comes your mother."

Our waitress snapped a menu off the empty table next to ours and put it into Theo's hand as she sat down. There was a stain the size of a grapefruit on Theo's blouse. "You guys eating already?" she said. "Couldn't wait, huh?"

"It's been ages, Mom," Rachel said.

Theo studied the menu for a second and then waved it at the waitress, who was standing next to Clare's table watching the short girl mop the floor. "Coffee and Peach Hawaiian," she said when the waitress arrived.

"Three coffees?" the waitress said to me. She pointed to

the second cup on the table, then looked back and forth from me to Theo.

"O.K. So just the pie. Sorry." The waitress left and Theo said, "Clare wonders why you never talk to her."

"You were talking," I said.

"Three people can't talk, right? You married the woman, after all."

"I barely remember," I said. That was true. The first time I saw Clare after the divorce we went for coffee and talked about things that had happened to us when we were married. The conversation was stiff. What we talked about seemed like things that had happened to somebody else. Since then I had avoided her.

"She remembers," Theo said. "And Joel says he wants to get to know you better."

"He looks like a you-know-what in that shirt," Rachel said.

"Eat," Theo said, pushing Rachel's head down close to the ice-cream bowl. She rolled her eyes and moved her lips in an imaginary prayer. "Anyway, Clare wants to come see the house. I get the feeling she and Joel aren't doing so great."

"Uh-huh," I said.

"What is that, Frank Furillo?"

I started to answer, but she put up her hand quick.

"No. Don't do it again. I'm just telling you about this in case anything happens."

The waitress arrived with Theo's pie, banged it down on the tan Formica, said, "That be it?" and, while we nodded, tore a check off her pad and stuck it into the chrome spring on top of the rack of sugar packets.

Theo ate her pie in three or four bites, then left the booth and went up to the counter to get something to go. Rachel hadn't touched her pecan pie. "That stuff's terrible," she said, poking the pie with a spoon. "I'm glad I didn't eat it."

I gave her a nasty look, and she said, "I know, I know.

People are starving all over the place. But, look at this."
She mashed the point of the pie, then flipped a few pecans
onto the tabletop. "They'd puke this stuff, wouldn't they?"

"That's very nice, Rachel," I said as we slid out of the
booth. "That's very attractive."

"Oh, Dad," she said.

WE BOUGHT a dog. I thought we ought to get a puppy, but Theo knew this breeder at the university, so we ended up with a German short-haired pointer, white and caramel, with a huge bark. "He's old, but he's still nice," Theo said the day she brought him home.

The dog's name was Albert, but we called him Harold, after Theo's brother, the hard-luck case in her family. Harold sold Cyclone fencing door-to-door in Big Spring, and was always getting attacked. We heard a lot about dogs ripping off arms and legs. On the day after we got Harold, he had a fight with Duncan Brown's dog, Jupiter. Harold won, so we had to apologize, which is something I don't mind doing, usually, because it makes everybody feel better. The fight started in our front yard, but we didn't get the dogs apart until they'd fought their way over into the Browns' driveway. I walked Harold to the house and locked him inside while Theo talked to Cindy Brown about the cuts on her dog, which was wrapped up in a ball under a bush at the edge of the drive. When I got back Theo was saying how sorry she was it had ever happened.

"I just can't believe it," I said, jumping the little hedge between our properties. "I feel horrible. We may have to do something about Harold, Theo. This is terrible. I mean, really, this is awful." I shook my head and shrugged at Cindy. "I'm so sorry. I thought those two would like each other."

It was only the third time I'd met Cindy Brown. She was standing alongside one of their two BMWs eating a chocolate bar and nervously eyeing the dog. "We named him after the planet," she said. "Duncan's crazy for planets."

"I'm really sorry," I said.

"He'll be all right," Theo said. "Don't you think, Cindy?"

"I don't know. There's something on his shoulder there."
She pointed the chocolate bar at Jupiter. "I don't know."

Theo and I were in the middle of an argument about
friends—she wanted some and she said I didn't. "You
just hide out all the time like a palooka," she'd said that
morning. "You got away with it at the apartment, but
you've got a house now. You've got neighbors. What about
the Browns?"

"What about them?" I said.

"I'm having them over," she said. "Formally, I mean."

"We already had him," I said. "He broke the chair, remember? But go ahead, I'm ready for anything." I thought
that was funny and romantic, something from a new movie
full of wood-sided station wagons and blue-green pools—
the kind of movie they started making a few years ago, in
which ordinary life is at once ridiculed and shown to be
strange and wonderful.

"I'm calling her," Theo had said. "They can be our
friends."

"Fine," I said.

Then the dogs had the fight. Theo hadn't called yet, and
when we walked back to our house after making sure Cindy
didn't want to get a vet, Theo said, "I'm still inviting them.
But I'm going to wait."

Cindy called the ASPCA. In the middle of the afternoon
a white city truck pulled up in front of our house and two
guys in identical orange shirts found Harold, whom I'd let
out, in the flowerbed by the driveway. I watched them check
Harold's tags, then walk him up to our door. When I answered the bell the taller of the two introduced himself and
told me he was going to have to take the dog to the pound
for tests. He didn't call it the pound. He called it the office.
"Routine stuff," he said. "Nothing to sweat."

"Is this about the fight?" I said.

"Yep," the shorter one said. He had a face shaped like a

football, a very dark tan, and bad skin. He flapped open an aluminum clipboard. "Reported by a Mrs. Brown." He poked his finger on Harold's skull a couple of times and said, "He don't look rabid, but the city says we got to check him out." Harold twisted his head around to look at the short guy, then took a swipe at the finger with his tongue. "Naw, hell— we look all right," the guy said, tugging on Harold's ear. "See that tongue? That's the best-looking tongue I've seen in weeks. Right, Hondo?"

"Right," the tall guy said. "That's a great tongue. So let's go. We've got the chow on Barna Place to get." He gave me a receipt and snapped a leash on Harold's collar. "You can get him anytime after four-thirty," he said. "They close at seven. Bring ten bucks, cash, no checks."

They put Harold in the back of the truck. I stayed on the porch and watched them go, then looked at Armstrong, across the street. He was out washing the side of his house with a hose and a push broom.

Theo had gone to get Rachel. When she got back, I told her about the ASPCA. She got mad and called Cindy. "Hello, Cindy," she said. "You had them take Harold? That's fine. It's so nice having neighbors. And, oh, please try to keep your nice puppy out of our drive, will you? I wouldn't want to smash his head into a ball of grease with my car tire." She slammed the phone into its cradle before Cindy had a chance to say anything.

I went to get Harold. The pound was a low concrete-block building diagonally across from the abandoned rail terminal. In the lobby a line of construction-paper sheets with glitter letters on them, one to the sheet, was tacked to the wall. The message was PETS ARE PRECIOUS, and it was signed on the last sheet by the fifteen members of the Doxiama Elementary School second grade. That included Debra and Bart and Nikki and Rosalie and Spider, among others. I was reading the names when a guy who looked like Bruce Dern came through a tin-covered door and asked me what I wanted. I told him.

"Oh yeah," he said, stripping off the oversize black rubber gloves he was wearing. He pulled an already open Baby Ruth out of his shirt pocket and took a bite. "Kind of a spotty? Looks like a hound dog, that him? Real friendly?"

"Sounds like Harold," I said.

We walked through another tin-covered door and into a narrow concrete-floored alley between two rows of damp, wire-fenced pens. Most of the dogs didn't look too bad, but the building looked like something you might see on *Nightly News*. Harold was in the next-to-last pen. "This him?" the guy said, slapping the gloves against the gate.

I said it was.

"Well, let's get him the hell out of here." He opened the gate and Harold came out running and jumping. Some kind of ratty little monkey skittered out from behind a dark-green fifty-gallon drum that was alongside the last pen, and the Bruce Dern guy gave the monkey a hand up onto his shoulder, then followed me and Harold all the way out to the parking lot. He was petting the monkey and feeding it bits of chocolate from the Baby Ruth. "Twenty bucks," he said, after I'd gotten Harold in the back seat.

I reached for my wallet. "Twenty?"

"You got hearing loss? Twenty."

I pulled out two ten-dollar bills and handed them to him. The monkey grabbed the bills and started chewing on them. The guy grinned. "Hungry monkey," he said.

After dinner Duncan Brown called and said my wife shouldn't threaten his wife. "Besides," he said. "I called the ASPCA. She didn't. Maybe I overreacted. I probably made him sound worse than he really is. You probably had to go over there, didn't you? To the pound, I mean. I'm really sorry."

"I just got back."

"I shouldn't have done it," he said. "I don't know what I was thinking of. Cindy called me at the office and I was in the middle of something, and—you know. It just got out of hand, Henry. I really feel rotten. It's not Harold's fault they got in the fight. I know that. Look, let's forget this one, O.K.? Let's just put it behind us. You people want to come for drinks Friday? We're having Jerry and Grace."

I put my palm over the telephone mouthpiece and asked Theo. She frowned, but then said, "I guess we'd better go." I got back on the phone and said, "Fine. Sounds fine."

"Tell him we'll bring Harold," Theo said. "Make it a kind of get-together for the dogs, so they can make up." She nodded seriously and pointed at the phone, so I asked Duncan.

"That a joke?" he said. "If that's a joke it's not funny."

"No joke," I said. "I mean, I think it's a good idea. Maybe they'll learn to get along."

He went to ask Cindy and then he was back on the phone saying she didn't think it would work, but if we wanted to do it we should come early, because if it didn't work she didn't want the party screwed up.

"We'll just take our dog and go home."

"Fine," Duncan said. "See you then."

That night I watched a TV movie about a Southern sheriff who was involved in white slavery. The movie spent a lot of time looking at thin young girls in plain gray dresses. About halfway through I went out to the kitchen. Theo was making a Black Bottom pie for somebody at her office. "This Friday thing," I said. "Taking Harold over and all that. He'll probably chew up that twit again."

Theo was grating a big semisweet chocolate bar. "I don't see how you can get out of it now, do you?"

There was a knock on the kitchen door. I opened it. Cindy was on the back porch, in the yellow light that's supposed to discourage bugs. Cindy looked bad. She was swatting at a moth that seemed to want to land in her hair.

I said, "Hi. Come in. What's the matter?"

"It's Jupiter," she said. "I think he got some infection from Harold, where Harold bit him." She made a little mouth with her hand and bit herself on the neck with it. "It's a mess. It's all swollen and purple. Duncan says I'll have to take Jupiter to the vet."

"That's terrible," Theo said.

"He'll be all right," I said. "I know a vet we can call tonight if you want."

Theo put a red mug of coffee in front of Cindy, who sat at the kitchen table thumbing a magazine. "Jupiter is so important to us," she said. "I know it's dumb, but he is."

"It's not dumb," Theo said. "Not at all. We know exactly what you mean, don't we, Henry?"

I looked in the drawer by the refrigerator for the card with the emergency numbers on it. "Sure do," I said. "We're dumb about Harold."

"It's just after what happened to the other one," Cindy said. "Blitzen. You remember? I told you about that this afternoon, didn't I?"

"Yes," Theo said. "I don't know why the men didn't notice that he was in that can. The way they toss those things around. He barked at trucks, didn't he?"

"Not the garbage truck," Cindy said. "He never barked at a garbage truck in his whole life. I don't know why."

"Don't worry," I said. "Dogs fight all the time. They get these bites on them and then, after a while, things heal up just like new."

"I hope they don't have to shave him," Theo said. "When they're all shaved up all I can think of is mange."

Cindy looked up from her coffee.

Theo shook her head. "I'm sure they won't have to, though. They don't do that much anymore."

I went to get my address book. Harold was on the bed,

sleeping with one paw over his nose. "You're cute," I said to him. I got the book and shut the bedroom door on my way out. Cindy was telling Theo about Key West. The Browns spent a week there last winter. They took Jupiter and he had a wonderful time in the sand. Duncan got sun poisoning and had to stay in the room the whole time, but Cindy and Jupiter went for long walks on the beach. Cindy waved each time she passed back and forth in front of the room. Once, Jupiter ran all the way up and clawed at the glass.

"I put the pie in the freezer," Theo said. "We can have a piece in a few minutes."

"I thought it was spoken for," I said.

She ignored me. "Do you want to call Duncan? See if everything's all right?"

"He's in bed with his sinuses," Cindy said. She looked at her watch, then pulled the stem and wound it. She was a small woman with careful black hair and pale eye shadow. Her wrists were the size of paper-towel tubes.

"Poor Duncan," Theo said. "Sinuses can really blow your face all out of whack." She went to the sink and ran water into the bowl she'd used for the chocolate.

"Between him and Jupiter I've got my hands full," Cindy said. "You think he'll be O.K.? Jupiter?"

"Sure," I said. I waved the address book. "Or we can call Wenzel. Theo's friend told us about this guy."

"He's great on the gall bladder," Theo said.

"You think something's wrong internally?"

"No, I didn't mean that," Theo said. She looked at me.

"Don't look at me," I said. "He's your employer."

"Stones, maybe it's stones," Cindy said. "That's not uncommon in today's dog."

"Is this pie ready yet?" I went to the refrigerator and opened the freezer door. The pie was lopsided on a tower of three or four Birdseye lima-bean packs. "Looks ready."

"He can tell by looking," Theo said to Cindy. "A rare gift." She crossed the kitchen and closed the freezer door.

"Not ready. I think it was stones, now that I remember it. Little stones no bigger than wood ticks. I thought he was going to die, swear to God."

"Who?" Cindy said.

Theo took the book from my hand and went back to the table. "Rocky here." She shot a thumb over her shoulder at me. "He's afraid of medicine. You should've seen him when I explained about worms. Get me a pencil, will you?" She leafed through the book, shaking her head.

I gave her a red felt-tip pen. She wrote Wenzel's number on a corner of the evening paper, then tore off the corner and handed it to Cindy.

The phone rang. It was Duncan calling to see if Cindy was with us. I told him she was and handed her the receiver. She made a face and took the phone.

Rachel came in through the back door carrying a jar with a toad in it. "I need an icepick," she said. "I've got to get some holes in here before this guy dies. Hi, Cindy," She started opening and closing drawers next to the sink.

"Third one up," Theo said.

Cindy was whispering into the receiver. She'd turned her back and had her forehead pressed against the small green chalkboard on the wall next to the phone.

Rachel got the icepick and squatted in the middle of the kitchen, struggling to push the point through the jar top. "I've got to save this creep for school," she said.

"You have to hit it," I said. I took the pick, steadied it, then popped it with the heel of my hand. The jar busted. Glass scattered all over the place. Rachel fell over backwards.

Theo said, "Oh, crap. Did she cut herself?"

The toad hopped toward the living room. Rachel went after it. "That's great, Dad," she said, over her shoulder. "That's really great."

"Well, help her, why don't you?" Theo said.

I started out of the room and heard Cindy say, "Henry tried to stick Rachel's frog."

We chased the toad around the living room for a few minutes, finally trapping it under the sofa. I told Rachel that I was going to lift the sofa and she should grab the toad. But when we tried that, she missed, and the toad went into the hall leading back to the bedrooms. Harold started barking and scratching at the bedroom door. Theo came down the hall from the kitchen. "Oh, get out of the way," she said. She grabbed the toad by one of its back legs. It jerked a couple of times as if trying to hop away, but then gave up and hung limp in her hand.

"Don't hurt his feet," Rachel said.

"I'm not hurting his feet," Theo said. "Get me something to put him in." She carried the toad back to the kitchen.

"What?" Rachel said. She ran around her mother and into the kitchen.

"How about a bowl?" I said.

"I don't want this frog in my bowls," Theo said. "Get the Tupperware thing out of the cabinet."

"Oh, yeah," Rachel said. "Great."

"You want me to put some holes in the top?" I said.

"Sure, Dad."

"I'll do the holes," Theo said. Cindy was still on the telephone. She turned to see what we were doing and the toad somehow jumped out of Theo's grip and landed on Cindy's chest. She jerked away, banging her head against the range hood. "Shit," she said, rubbing the spot.

"Shit?" Rachel said.

Theo picked up the toad.

"I've got to go, Duncan," Cindy said into the phone. "Theo put a frog on me."

Harold was still barking. "Shut him up, will you?" Theo said. "I don't know why he thinks he has to bark at everything. What good does it do?"

"Jupiter's getting worse," Cindy said, hanging up the phone. "He went under the house and Duncan had to go under there after him. I think we'd better call the vet."

"Take care of him, please," Theo said to me, waving toward the bedroom.

I yelled down the hall for Harold to be quiet.

"What's the vet's number?" Theo said, dropping the toad into an orange Tupperware bowl Rachel was holding. I handed her the paper she'd written the number on and she started for the phone.

"Is the pie ready?" Rachel said. "I want some pie to watch TV with."

"The pie's not ready," Theo said.

"Maybe you could take Harold out in the backyard for a run," I said to Rachel. "He sounds like he wants to go out."

"He wants to eat my frog like last time, remember?"

"I'm going to eat it if you don't get it out of here," Theo said.

I opened the Browns' door when Wenzel rang. He was twenty, wearing a Jim Morrison tee shirt. He had a carefully trimmed gray stubble on his chin and thick glasses with red frames. "Where's the pup?" he said. He hoisted a bag big enough for a couple of bowling balls off the rubber mat and followed Cindy into the kitchen.

"Forget Friday," Theo whispered to me. "It stinks in here. I don't think these people ever wash. We'll pretend we forgot. Maybe we'll go away for the weekend."

We sat in the Browns' living room and waited for Cindy and Wenzel to reappear. The room was decorated with thickly padded furniture, heavy drapes, deep-pile carpet. I counted six different floral prints, including two on the walls. Even the coffee table had a flower motif around the edge. Everything in the room had been wrapped in foam or flowers. I was looking around and Theo was staring at the single uncovered window when Duncan came in bundled in a gold sheet.

"Howdy," he said. "The doc here?"

"With the patient," I said. I pointed toward the hall that led to the kitchen.

"I've been napping," Duncan said. He stood in the open arch between the living and dining rooms holding the sheet from underneath with two hands. I could see his fists outlined in the cloth. "I guess Harold's had his shots?"

Theo and I nodded.

"I was sure he had," Duncan said. "It's really not all that serious. Just a lump on his neck, right about here." He brought the lower hand out from the sheet and made a biting motion on the back of his neck. The sheet came open. He was wearing boxer shorts, tan, with a double pin stripe. He glanced down and quickly closed the sheet by turning his body to one side. Then he drew his hand back under the sheet and said, "Sorry, Theo."

"It's O.K.," she said.

"Can I get you something? Beer?"

She shook her head and I said, "No, thanks," then the three of us were quiet for a minute.

Theo got up. "We're not much good here." She looked at me and I got up, too. "I'm going to see if I can help. This vet is somebody somebody suggested, we don't really know him. I mean, we've used him, but he didn't look too great." She started for the kitchen.

Duncan shuffled across the carpet. "Good idea. Me and Henry need to talk anyway." When Theo was out of sight he grabbed my arm and pulled me back onto the couch. "All the women I ever slept with were lousy lovers," he said. "I thought it was me, but I asked Bert and he said it was the same for him. That's the kind of thing he always says."

"Bert?" I said.

"My analyst," Duncan said. "You'll meet him at dinner Friday. He's a short guy with a mustache. Plays racquetball with me."

"He's your analyst?"

"Well, therapist. Bert says celibacy's not such a bad thing."

"Uh-huh," I said.

"You know, when I was a kid I played priest all the time. I'd make an altar out of a cardboard box covered with a sheet. My mother had this pewter cup I used for a chalice, and I used the *Columbia Encyclopedia* for a missal. I had vestments, salad-dressing things for cruets, smashed bread for the host. You do that? Cut bread circles with a glass and mash them?"

"Sure," I said. "Did it yesterday."

"I spent a lot of afternoons genuflecting and raising the host—once I went for a week holding my thumbs and forefingers together the way priests do. Mother didn't discourage it. I think she figured it was cowboys and Indians."

I nodded and smiled and looked at the backs of my hands, then at the door leading into the kitchen.

"Priests have it good," Duncan said. "They get those robes—do they still wear those? I always envied priests."

"I don't think they do anymore," I said. "Reforms. Modernization."

"God helps those bastards right off the planet, you know what I'm saying, Henry?" Duncan put his hand on my knee for emphasis. "They go around feeling good all the time. I mean, what are a priest's problems? A priest wants a good meal, a couple of drinks, a television set."

"Basketball," I said. "They always like basketball."

"Right. Right. You know, if we still had Del—you knew we had a boy that died, didn't you? His name was Del. Anyway, we talked about schools and everything, before the accident. We thought about St. Pius, but Cindy wasn't happy. I guess we would have looked at some other schools. I wanted him in a Catholic school, but I get the feeling they aren't what they were. I mean, I had to go to class for six weeks in the convent in the fifth grade because I threw something at this pig of a nun who lied to the mother superior about me, told her I'd made remarks about her sexual apparatus—no kidding, that's what she called it. They assigned me a room in the convent for six weeks. Somebody brought me the lessons every afternoon, and the next day I sat in that dark little room staring out the window at the baseball diamond. It's a good thing I like baseball."

The dog squealed in the kitchen and Duncan winced. I said, "You think we ought to see what's going on?"

"Naw," he said. "You know the guy, right? Anyway, it isn't that bad." Duncan waved the sheet around his legs a couple of times, then grabbed my knee again. "I had a teacher named Sister Mary Phantom. Incredible. She went around in that habit, wooden rosary beads clicking and everything, those black shoes, all that stiff white stuff surrounding her face—God knows what she really looked like. Now they look like the girls at the grocery store. It's horrible."

I shrugged and stood up. "I know. There's some bad stuff going on."

"You said it," Duncan said. "I mean, the priests now, they don't even *smell* like they used to."

"Guitars," I said.

Theo and Cindy and Wenzel came into the living room single file. Theo pulled her thumb over her shoulder. "Let's go, Henry. The worst is over."

"Is Jupiter all right?" Duncan asked. He stood up beside me.

"Perfect," Wenzel said.

Cindy put her arm around Duncan. "Dr. Wenzel gave him a shot so he could sleep. No problem." She patted her husband's shoulder.

I sidestepped the coffee table and shuffled out the door with Theo and Wenzel. "Nobody wants to stay for coffee?" Cindy said when the three of us were on the porch.

We thanked her and said no, and she thanked Wenzel, and Duncan said it was real nice to have somebody to talk to once in a while, and then the three of us started for the street. The door closed behind us and the porch light went off. We stopped at Wenzel's car to thank him for coming and he said, "You'd better bring yours around, too. He's got bite problems. Molar distortion."

———— • ————

C LARE CAME to see the new house. The three of us
sat in the living room. Rachel was in front of the
television, watching a game show on the religious channel.

"I've got that fan for you," I said, pointing to an oscillating
fan that was standing on a flattened grocery bag in one
corner of the room. The fan belonged to her.

She played with her purse. "Oh, great. Thanks. I thought
I'd come over now because Joel's working. Are you getting
furniture, or are you sticking with the Japanese look?"

We had a beat-up Empire couch, a modern rug I got
from my father, and two bentwood chairs in the living room.
In the kitchen we had a dining table, a fifties aluminum-
and-linoleum thing that Theo liked more than I did.

"Henry's building a new table with these great old legs,"
Theo said. "How come Joel's working tonight?"

"They're making him take this sensitivity-training se-
quence out at the college, some guy named Polop—you
know him?"

"I know him," I said.

"Joel needs some kind of training," Clare said. She looked
at her hands, then bent to look at Theo's new copy of
Fitness, tracing her finger around the hip of the woman on
the cover. "You look good, Henry. I was surprised when I
saw you at Pie Country. You look healthy." She went into
the kitchen and opened the refrigerator.

Theo smiled at me.

Clare poured milk from a red carton into a wineglass.

"You shouldn't drink milk," I said. "I read a piece somewhere that said milk'll kill you."

38

She came to the kitchen door still holding the milk carton. "I saw Dr. Lima. He's got a new nurse you'd like. Blue nails and she smells like flowers." She came back into the room holding the glass with two hands.

"He's back on the dental assistant," Theo said. "I like the pants. That's a new look, isn't it?" Clare was wearing parachute pants. With one hand Theo flapped the extra fabric at Clare's hip.

"You think I can get away with it?"

"Sure," Theo said. "Why are you so tall all of the sudden? What've you got, six-inch heels?"

Clare grinned at Theo, then stared at me, gently rocking the milk back and forth in the wineglass. "My Love-Is-Just-Another-Name-for-Napalm spikes," she said.

Rachel said, "Great. The TV's messed up." She tugged at my arm. "You want to fix it?"

"You can get rid of those," Clare said as I headed for the TV. She pointed to the drapes. "Somebody thought they were artistic. They look like Nassar's top-of-the-line."

Nassar was a guy who ran an apartment project Clare and I had lived in for a couple of months after we were married, and where she was now living with Joel.

Clare shut her eyes and shook her head, then went into the bathroom, leaving the door open. Her heels snapped on the tile floor. She turned on the water in the lavatory. "Are you going to paint?"

"He wants to do the whole house in khaki," Theo said. "Maybe you can talk him out of it."

"What?" Clare stuck her head into the doorway. "This is the same soap. Blue soap. I always hated this soap. How can you stand this soap, Theo?"

"Joel doing O.K.?" I said.

She turned off the water and came back into the living room. "You already know, I think." She took a drink from the wineglass and got a white comb of milk on her top lip. "At least you've got a house. That's worth something, isn't it?" She slumped into the couch and started chipping polish off her nails with a credit card. The polish dropped in bright-red flakes on her blouse, which was black and looked like silk. "Let's get us some Mexican food to celebrate." She scratched the card up her calf, then pointed to the television. The picture was shaking and slowly rolling over. "Fix that or turn it off, will you?"

I pulled the set away from the wall and started fiddling with the controls on the back. "Can you see it? Tell me when it quits."

"I'll tell you," Theo said. "Worse—wait. That was better for a minute. Back up. Now go real slow, easy—there. No, you had it before. Go back the other way. This bushy-haired woman is way ahead. She's got a hundred nineteen."

"That's a thousand and nineteen, Mom."

"She looks like her jaw's wired shut," Clare said.

"What about the picture?" I bent over the set, looking at the screen. The picture was divided in half, the top on the bottom and the bottom on top.

"I remember this TV," Clare said. "It never did work right. One time I watched a whole movie like that. Bill Holden. That one where he's dead in the pool. You were in New Mexico or something."

I pushed the set back into place.

Theo stretched out and pulled on the chain of the floor lamp, but nothing happened. "Where's the light?" she said, getting up to take a closer look.

"I may try to stay away from Joel for a while," Clare said. "Just to see how it is."

"I've wanted to do that," Theo said. "Just to clean things out, right? But Henry would probably understand me to death, he understands everything." She looked quickly at me. "Anyway, it comes up so often we don't take it seriously. Maybe you can stay over. I could use the company some-times."

"Chopped liver over here," I said, taking a bottle of aspirin out of my pants pocket. I rattled the pills in her direction.

THE HOUSE on Palm Avenue was one we had noticed but never been inside—a bungalow, built in the forties, smaller than the others on its block, gray, with a screen porch and carpenter-Gothic trim. Theo said she wanted to look, at least. Rachel, Theo's thirteen-year-old, said she liked the apartment and didn't see the big deal about a house. I agreed with Rachel. "It's got a new sign, a For Sale by Owner sign," Theo said, pulling a scrap of paper out of her purse. She called the people and said we were on our way. Rachel didn't want to go.

The owners were a clean-looking couple named Jerry and Grace Kluge, in their mid-twenties, about ten years younger than us. "Jerry built the fireplace himself," Grace said. "We had the wall over here covered with tarps for about six weeks." She wiggled a hand toward the fireplace, which was brick, but had a modern look to it.

"It's fully functional," Jerry said. He patted his wife's head. "Grace did a lot of work on it, too."

"It's cute," Theo said. "The house, I mean. How big is it, exactly?"

"Runs fourteen hundred square feet," Grace said. "Not counting the porch."

I put a toe on one of the bricks in the fireplace and the brick slipped, making a sandpapery sound.

"Oops!" Jerry said, grinning at me as he squatted to push the brick back into place. "You found him."

"He calls it his secret friend," Grace said.

Jerry clicked his tongue and shook his head. "Thanks, Grace," he said.

"Well, you do," she said.

She closed her eyes and said something to herself.

The doorbell went off and Clare jumped, splashing milk on her pale, shiny calves. Joel was on the porch, looking in. He was wearing a suit and he had a fire-red Adidas tote in his hand. He leaned against the door, pushing it open, and jerked the bag at me a couple of times. "What are we doing? Is that Clare?"

"Hello, Joel," she said.

"I guessed you'd be here," he said. He dropped the tote into my hand.

Joel was not happy. All through dinner, which Rachel and I went to fetch at Border Bill's, a drive-in enchilada place, he baited Clare, made jokes about her, ridiculed her. It was easy to see why she wanted to get away.

Joel and Clare left right after the meal. I carried dishes out and then sat in the kitchen watching Theo wash. "It's hard to feature them together," she said.

"He's funny, sometimes. He was funny once, in an ugly way."

"I don't think he's funny," she said.

At midnight the doorbell rang. I got out of bed and answered the door. Clare was outside the screen in tears. "I need to stay here tonight. Is that O.K.?"

"Of course. Come on." I opened the screen for her, then tried to put my arm around her, but she twisted away.

Theo came out of the bedroom. I sat with the two of them for twenty minutes, then I went into the back. Theo came in after half an hour. "I bedded her down on the couch," she said. "The guy's a jerk, but I don't want to be in the middle."

"I know," I said. I was arranging a towel over my eyes— I sleep with a towel over the top of my head and down over my eyes to keep out the morning light. Theo says she can't understand it.

"You don't mind her staying, do you?"

"As long as you stay, too," I said. "To protect me, I mean. Joel's probably outside right now, crawling around in the bushes. Ready to torch the place."

She stood by the window for a minute, pulling the shade out so she could look into the yard. "I don't see him." She got into bed and cupped her hand around my bare thigh. "So. Big Boy," she said.

J ERRY AND Grace didn't go to Arkansas. He got a job
teaching French horn in the music department at the
university, and Grace decided she hated history and Arkansas. "It's probably the worst department in the civilized
world, anyway," she said when they dropped by a month
after we'd moved in. "The job they told me was tenure track
turned out to be terminal, one year. We got an apartment
at Madeline Place. Around the corner."

Madeline Place was a complex on ten wooded acres the
university had recently sold to pay for a fabulous new football stadium. It had cantilevered balconies, trapezoidal roofs,
huge plates of glass, three pools, tennis courts, saunas, dance
studio, gymnasium, twenty-four-hour security—all for
thirty-six sets of young well-to-do residents. As my last gasp
before we bought the house I took Theo by for a look, but
she just laughed at me, said it was a freak show and she
wouldn't live there on borrowed money. "We looked there,"
I said. "I think it's wonderful."

"Everybody does," Jerry said. "They're turning condo
next year and we're definitely buying in."

"I wouldn't do it if I were you," Theo said. "Without the
ground you got nothing. The ground is what you want."

"Yeah, I used to think that," he said.

Clare had been with us since the Mexican dinner with
Joel. When she breezed into the house and introduced
herself as my ex-wife, Jerry and Grace were uneasy.

"It's O.K.," Theo said. "Don't worry about it. Clare likes
me better than she likes him."

"I'm afraid that's true, Henry," Clare said.

43

"They torture me," I said. "I like it pretty much."

"I'll drink to that," Jerry said, raising the Stroh's bottle he'd brought with him. "So, look, why don't we head over to our place for a swim?"

"We got a thigh problem over here," Theo said. "We swim in Bermuda shorts only."

"Oh, don't be silly," Grace said. She reached out and patted Theo's bare knee. "They take whatever we give them these days."

"I don't know what she's talking about," Jerry said. "It's all these faggots she hangs out with. They turn her brain to mush. Make her think she's a real person."

Theo slid back on the sofa and propped her feet on my knee. "What's all this faggot talk? Two weeks ago Rachel was on a binge and now you guys."

"Jerry thinks gay girls are wonderful," Grace said. "He gets to look at them, but he doesn't have to do anything."

"That's original," Theo said, glancing at me.

Jerry hung his head. "She's got me pegged, all right. My own wife revealing a cruel and personal truth."

"He just discovered them," she said. "One of our neighbors is that news girl from Channel Fourteen."

"She's gay?" Clare said. "Caitlin Smith—is that her name?"

"That's her," Jerry said. "And even more beautiful by the pool than behind that stupid desk they make her sit at."

"Jerry doesn't like her desk," Grace said.

"She doesn't like it," he said. "I can tell just by looking at her that she thinks it's cruddy."

"It's not a great desk," I said. "From an interior-design standpoint."

"That's the only standpoint we ever use around here," Theo said. "As you can see." She waved a hand in a half-circle, showing off the room.

"So what's this about a swim?" Clare said. "My thighs are fine."

"Oh, don't be such a slut, Clare," Theo said.

* * *

We moved some furniture so Clare could take over the study. She bought a single bed and we moved in an extra dresser from Rachel's room, and then she didn't stay around much. She was out with Joel trying to patch things up. They worked too hard—museums and late-night country drives, weekday trips to the beach, specialty shops and foreign cookies. He was maudlin and sheeplike, and she was too eager, and the unease rubbed off on us.

"What do you think?" Clare asked us one night at dinner. Joel had gone out of town the night before, a business trip, and she had promised to make a decision about moving in with him again.

"I think he's only being nice so he can get what he wants," Rachel said. "I know a lot of boys like that."

"Me too," Clare said, eyeing me. "Thank you, Rachel."

"Don't look at me," I said.

"Don't you have some Fortran to study or something?" Theo said to Rachel.

"Mom, it's not Fortran. It's BASIC, and if you want me to shut up and leave the room the least you can do is say so."

"Fine," Theo said. "Please shut up and leave the room."

Rachel pushed her chair away from the table. "That's cute, Mom. You should know that I read in *Time* that sixty-seven percent of the children of two-income families have computers." She took her plate into the kitchen, and, on her way back through the dining room, said, "Those kids will have a big advantage over guys like me when the time comes to enter the work force."

"You saw that on television," I said.

"So what's the difference?" Rachel said. "I think you should stay, Clare. I don't like him."

Clare said, "Thanks, Chief."

When Rachel was gone Theo said, "I like having you, Clare. You take my mind off things."

"Henry?" Clare said.

"For one," I said. "No, sorry. It's great with me. Stay a lifetime."

I'd married Clare when she was twenty-two and knew what she wanted. We were married less than a year. She took off with a kid who made jewelry and sold it off a card table at flea markets. She wrote me a long letter, apologizing, describing herself as a simpleminded piece of ass. She even called a couple of times—once from Arizona, once from California—to see how I was getting along, how I was taking it. I was taking it badly. I cried a lot. I went to church and prayed—give me cancer, take off a leg, anything, just bring her back. It didn't work. Three months later I got divorce papers in the mail, along with a return envelope addressed to her in Kenosha, Wisconsin. I looked at the papers for a week, and then I signed.

"C'mon, Henry," Theo said. "Why don't you ever say what you mean?"

"I do," I said. "I just don't mean much. If Clare wants to stay, it's O.K. with me. That's what I mean in this case."

"He's an easygoing type of guy," she said to Clare. "Now that he's a big executive nothing interesting ever happens to him."

"That's a figure of speech," I said. "The executive part."

Clare twisted the curls around her ear. "I don't know what I should do. I don't know what Joel will do if I stay."

"He can move in, too," Rachel said. She was passing through, on her way to the kitchen.

"Funny, Rachel," Clare called after her.

"Now," I said. "Here's an issue."

Theo gave me a dirty look.

"He wants to buy that place on the corner," Clare said. She waved in the direction of the Browns' house. "Not this corner. Palm and Fourth."

"That's a nice house," Theo said. "The peach brick one, right?" She looked at her fingers.

"I hate the idea myself," Clare said.

"So stay," I said. "We'll be a domestic-unit-of-the-eighties."

Theo rubbed her face with her palm, then shook her head.

"What," I said. "You don't want me around?"

They watched me get up and stick my hands into the pockets of my slacks. I stood there, waiting for an answer. I went out in the backyard and looked at the trees. In a few minutes, Duncan Brown came over the fence, a cedar job that Jerry had started to enclose his yard. "Howdy," Duncan said. He was wearing a black baseball hat.

"New hat?"

He stopped halfway across the yard, removed the hat, held it at arm's length and looked at it. "Yeah," he said. "I know what you mean." He balled the hat and then squatted down and rubbed in the dirt at the base of Theo's prize bush—one she'd bought at the A&P the night we closed on the house.

"I was just asking," I said.

"It takes a while to break them in. Cindy just brought it home and I'm trying it out."

I offered him a drink, but he didn't want one. He said he was working on his stomach, the inside. "I think Pepto Bismol has given us a false sense of security."

"Sometimes a good idea," I said.

"I read an article about antacids. Scared the hell out of me—I mean, can you imagine what goes on in there?" He pointed to his stomach. "All that lurching and spasming?" He sat down on the deck alongside me. He was a small guy, less than six feet, probably less than five-eight. Where we were sitting his brown running shoes didn't even touch the ground.

"I don't want to hear anything about baseball," I said. "I hate baseball."

"Me too." He was swinging his legs back and forth. He put his hands, palms down, under his legs just above the knees. "Where's Theo?"

"She's in there deciding Clare's future."

He took the hat off and played with it. "Clare's nice. She's what I want to talk about. Don't tell me if you don't want to. Really. You don't have to. But, you know, the neighborhood talks. Everybody wants to know." He grinned at me, but it wasn't an ugly grin. "I mean, Henry—are you sleeping with both of them?"

I smiled and slapped Duncan on the back. "Nope," I said. "Just one."

———— • ————

SATURDAY MORNING I got on a pair of shorts and a sleeveless sweatshirt and I went out and mowed the lawn for the first time. I used Duncan's mower, a state-of-the-art job from Sears. The sun was bright but not too hot, much cooler than usual in early fall. Theo spent the morning carrying a spade around the yard, testing the soil. I wondered what she was doing, but I didn't stop to ask. After I cleaned up I found out—she was in the backyard digging a hole. I got dressed, got a Diet Pepsi out of the refrigerator, and went out to the porch. "What's this about? Whatever you're doing out here. What are you doing, anyway?"

"Digging," she said.

"Oh," I said, surveying the work I'd done. I had missed a foot-wide strip by the fence. "What are you digging?"

"Nothing. I just feel like it. Where's Rachel?"

"She went somewhere with the Farmer kid. Are you planting something, or what? You want some help?"

"I don't know yet," she said. She straightened and pushed the long-handled spade into the grass alongside the hole she'd started. She wiped her hand through her hair, which was tangled and shooting out in different directions from her head.

I'd noticed that Theo was picking up Clare's mannerisms—looks, gestures with her eyes, ways of standing that had, in Clare years ago, reminded me of pictures my father had taken of my mother. Now, standing in the yard with one hand on her hip and the other wrapped around the top of the shovel's handle, Theo could've passed for my mother at thirty-five. Even more strange, I thought I remembered a picture of my mother in exactly that pose, with the same kind of shovel, standing in the yard of our house on Belvedere Drive. "You look like Mother," I said.

Theo squinted at me, raising the hand off her hip to shade her eyes. "I do?"

"You know that picture where they're putting down the bricks for the terrace? Just like it."

"What picture?"

"You've seen the picture. Her hair's sticking out. It looks like nineteen forty in the background."

"Is it sticking out?" she said, pushing at her hair. "Your mother's hair was longer than this."

"It's the same kind of thing."

"Uh-huh." She yanked her spade out of the ground and placed its blade carefully at the edge of the small hole.

"So, why are you digging up the lawn, Theo? I just mowed it, you know."

She sighed dramatically. "Yes, I know that, Henry." She pushed the shovel into the ground with her foot. "I don't know, it's something I like. Don't worry about it."

"Theo," I said.

She pulled a red cowboy neckerchief out of her pocket and mopped her brow, the shovel still stuck in the ground. "What? Did you want something?"

"I was thinking we might have lunch."

"It's not time," she said. "Besides, I've got some energy left." She waved the neckerchief at the sky. "Why don't you watch TV? Or read a book." She carried a shovel-load of dirt to the small pile she'd started near the fence.

"Gee, thanks." I watched her dig for a few more minutes, then went inside. The television was on in the living room. I sat on the couch and watched for a few minutes, a marathon, a lot of ordinary-looking people plodding through some pretty countryside, California I think it was.

Cindy called. "Hi. How are you?" she said.

"Fine," I said.

"Listen, I just wanted to tell you about this sale at Radio

Shack. We were over there. You know how you're always talking about the Intelevision I got Duncan? Well, they're on sale at Radio Shack for a hundred thirty-nine ninety-five. Can you believe it? I paid three fifty."

"I'm sorry," I said.

"It's all right because they're selling the cartridges too. I think they're closing out all their Intelevision stock. We got eighty or ninety dollars' worth of games for twenty-eight dollars."

"That's great. What'd you get?"

"Snafu. Frog Bog. Duncan got Dungeons and Dragons, one of those. I got this kid's word game for Rachel. It's cute. Monkeys running around with letters of the alphabet caught in their tails."

"Uh-huh." I was watching a pretty young girl with black hair and crimson shorts cross the finish line on television. "Sounds like you made a killing."

"I told Duncan we ought to have you guys over to play some of these, you know, make a party of it, but he said you wouldn't be interested."

"We're interested. We'll come over there and play for hours, days. What kind of joystick have you got? Oh, I guess the ones that came with the system, right?"

"I don't know," she said. "Does that make a difference?"

The marathon girl was bent at the waist, her hands on her knees, panting hard. She straightened and started walking in lopsided circles. The camera came in tight on her face. I could see the down on her cheek and the big bubbles of perspiration. "First we have to get Theo out of the backyard," I said. "She's out there digging a hole."

"Yeah, I saw her out there. What's she doing, anyway? Is she planting something or what?"

"I asked her that. She said she wasn't."

"Everything O.K. over there, Henry? I mean, marriage and family life and everything?"

"Perfect and beautiful," I said. A second runner, a woman

with light-brown hair and thousands of freckles, had come up behind the winner and touched her arm. They faced each other and then closed into an embrace.

"Well, it's great exercise. Digging, I mean. Does great things for the upper arms. Maybe I'll go out and see what she's up to."

"Call me back if you uncover anything, O.K.? I'll be in here watching this race on television, this marathon."

"Call you back," she said. "You're watching a marathon?"

"I'm not watching watching. I'm just looking at it."

"Even so," she said. "Anyway, I'll go talk to Theo. If you want to play some Frog Bog, just come on. O.K.? It's nice talking to you, Henry."

"You too," I said, but she had already hung up the phone. I remembered that Cindy always finished her telephone conversations abruptly. Theo had remarked on it when she was talking to Cindy about schools. I decided that the next time I talked to Cindy on the phone I'd hang up first. I dropped the receiver back into its cradle.

I got a banana from the kitchen, peeled it, then stood off to one side of the sink watching Theo hoist a shovel of dirt and toss it toward the pile. I heard Cindy shout at her, "Hey! Ease up, there, Tiger."

I tried to hear their conversation after Cindy came through the fence into our yard, but I could only pick up bits and pieces. They sat down in the grass. Theo put her feet into the hole she'd dug. Then I really couldn't hear what they were saying, so I dumped the last two inches of banana, wiped my hands on Theo's prized Ritz-A-Dish dishrag, and went in to take a nap.

Theo dug more on Sunday. She got up late, went out for an hour in the morning, took a lunch break around two, then went back outside in the afternoon. I watched a game on TV, getting up every couple of commercials to keep an eye on Theo. At the halftime of the second televised game Rachel caught me looking out the back window. "What's going on?" she said. "What's Mom doing out there?"

"Why don't you ask her?" I moved away from the window and put my arm around Rachel, walking her back to the living room.

"I already did, but I thought I'd better ask you, since you're sneaking around so much the last couple of days."

"Who is? Must be two other guys." I pointed to the television. "I'm watching this game. It's terrible. Where's Clare? Still not home from last night?"

"Clare never comes home. And I don't know why you call it home, anyway."

"Figure of speech."

"Well, since you don't want to tell me what Mom's doing or why you're sneaking around, maybe you want to look at this?" She handed me a copy of *Creative Computing*. "I got it from Julio. It has these comparisons of all the cheap computers and everything."

"O.K.," I said.

"It's the buyer's-guide issue. I read it already. I can't decide whether we should get a IIc or a Kaypro. Really the only one I don't want is the Timex thing."

"What's wrong with the Timex?" I said, flipping through the magazine.

"Membrane keyboard," she said. "It's impossible. Julio had one before he got his Apple, and he showed me. The keyboard is a hot zone in the interface between man and machine."

"Right. Nothing with a membrane keyboard. Are there any other specifications?" I went into the kitchen and looked at Theo shoveling dirt out of the hole, which was, by now, four feet across and a couple of feet deep.

"We need one hundred twenty-eight K," Rachel said. "You can't do anything without that. More would be better. Disk drives. Don't let anybody sell you a cassette, O.K.?

Probably a dot matrix printer, but a fully formed character printer if we're getting into word processing. Something with high-res graphics. Are you listening?"

"How about Frog Bog?" I said.

"That's a stupid copy of Frogger, Dad. You've got to read up on this stuff. You ought to see the neat way Julio does his homework. He wrote this BASIC program to figure out all the math problems."

"Julio's a big help. Who is he, anyway? One of these cute computer kids we always see on TV? You're going around with him since the Richie Farmer debacle?"

"I don't know what a debacle is. Julio hangs out with Richie. That's where I see him."

"A debacle is playing doctor at age thirteen."

She clicked her tongue in her teeth. "Right, Dad. Sure it is." She made more noises and pushed at the magazine. "Maybe you're ready to tell me about Mom? I mean, why is she digging and all that? I went out and asked her and she said she was looking for love in all the wrong places—what kind of thing is that to say to a kid my age?"

"Funny?"

"Not very," Rachel said, pulling open the refrigerator. "She told me you were buying a P-38 and she was looking for love. I don't get it. Isn't that some kind of old airplane?"

"Yeah. But I'm not buying one. You don't have to worry about it."

"I wasn't," Rachel said. She was chewing a huge strawberry she'd gotten out of the refrigerator. "Not about that, anyway."

Theo stuck her head in the door. "Hand me a beer, will you, Henry? It's hot out here."

"Hi, Mom," Rachel said. "Find anything?"

Theo gave Rachel a look and then snapped her fingers at me. I hadn't moved. "You're not telling her anything, are you?"

"That's great, Mom. Thanks a lot. That goes great with what you said outside."

"She's telling me," I said. "I think we're going to have to buy her a mainframe." I got a bottle of beer and started to twist off the top.

"I can handle it," Theo said. "Let's go, let's go." She wiggled her hand at me to tell me to hurry up and give her the bottle. When I handed it to her she got the top off and tossed it at the garbage, missing by a mile. She took a long drink. "The P-38 was really my father," she said to Rachel. "Not him." She pointed at me with the beer bottle. "He bought this scrap airplane. He didn't have it long. They brought it on a giant truck, you know the kind I'm talking about? They had the wings off and everything. Dumped it in the front yard and my mother went right through the roof. He told her it was an investment, but she told him to get it the hell out of there—it's one of the stories he used to tell.

"So what happened, Mom?"

"Then he told Mother he'd bought it for the kids in the neighborhood. She didn't buy that either. Really he just wanted it himself."

"Uh-huh," Rachel said. She'd gotten another strawberry and was eating it no-handed, holding the berry between her teeth so that the small leaves spread out like palm fronds in front of her mouth.

"I was only four or five," Theo said. "Harold used to camp out in the cockpit, he and his friends. My brother Harold. I think my father paid him to do that, that's the story, anyway. My father took these movies—we have them somewhere, packed away I guess. I remember this one scene with this ordinary-looking street, all nicely mowed and trimmed, everything so neat, and the camera goes around as if it's a very serious shot—to show the neighborhood, you know what I'm saying?"

"Kind of an establish shot?" Rachel said.

Theo took another drink, looking down the length of the bottle at Rachel. "Right. An establish shot. Anyway, it turns out he's filming from our driveway, so when the airplane

finally appears it's real big, taking up the whole screen—I
mean it's so huge it's out of focus. And there's my mother
with her hands on her hips, standing just off to one side of
the nose, and she's talking. It's a silent movie, but you can
tell by the way she looks she's telling him how stupid the
whole thing is. There are these neighbors in the backround,
the woman who lived next door, I think it was, and her
husband, and they're kind of craned around, looking to see
what's happening over at our house."

"I've never seen it, I don't think," Rachel said.

I hadn't seen it, either, although I'd heard the story.

"It's here somewhere," Theo said, gazing over her shoulder into the backyard. "I've got it packed away."

"So is that why you're digging the hole?" Rachel said. "I
still don't get it. What happened to the plane?"

"Killed my mother," Theo said.

Rachel put her hands on her head and looked at the
ceiling in dramatic exasperation. "Really funny, Mom."

"True," Theo said. "She had a heart attack and died
before he could get rid of the plane. We buried her in the
backyard—now do you get it?"

"That's disgusting," Rachel said. "I don't know why you
tell me stuff like that."

"Because she loves you," I said.

Theo finished the beer and put the bottle on the drainboard, wiping her mouth with the back of her hand. "No,
that's not it. I have an investment in the child."

"That's me," Rachel said.

"Right. A mother has to teach her daughter things, and
that's what I'm doing."

"Great," Rachel said. "You guys are weird. I think I'll
go over to Richie's house now."

"I'll read this computer magazine," I said, waving the
rolled-up magazine at Theo. "Everything we need to know,
right in here."

"I'm going back to work," Theo said. She pushed open

the back door. "You'd better bring in dinner, Henry. I just want a salad."

Rachel and I went to get fried fish at Long John Silver's. The evening sky was gray and close. It hadn't rained, but it looked as if it had. The light was even and filtered-looking. The streets we drove through were nicely kept, the lawns mowed and the shrubs clipped, the white driveways clean, the cars dustless and correctly parked. Rachel said, "Are you guys just fooling around? I mean, you know what I mean? Clare, and everything? I guess it's O.K., but it's pretty weird. Sometimes I wish I had regular parents like everybody else. It's scary."

"Don't be silly, Rachel. We're regular."

"You know what I mean."

We stopped at a traffic light, and I thought of Greg Tofurt, a boy with whom I often spent Friday nights when I was a kid. He lived in a subdivision north of the one we lived in. All the houses in his were ranch style. Brick, single story, with dens and glass doors opening on round concrete patios. Saturday mornings when we got up, the TV was always on, the washer going, Mr. Tofurt already out in the garage—we sat on high chrome-legged stools in the kitchen, eating heated rolls, drinking cold chocolate milk, while Greg's mother, who was much younger than my mother, carried things in and out of the laundry room, stopping occasionally to freshen her coffee and stare out the long window over the sink. She had perfect olive skin, dark glittery eyes, an aqua satin robe that never seemed to fully close. She had been a model before she married and wore no makeup except lipstick—a thick, wet red that made her lips glisten like tiny pillows carefully plumped and arranged. She was never without the lipstick.

Rachel poked me in the arm and said we were going to miss the light if we didn't move.

"What are the Farmers like?" I said, pressing the ball of my foot on the accelerator. "What's Mr. Farmer do, anyway?"

"He's a health nut," Rachel said. "He has a store in the mall. You know the one? Sports Stuff?"

"That's Richie's father?" I looked at Rachel. She was drumming her fingers on her jaw. "The guy in the running outfit? How come you didn't tell me?"

"I didn't want to because you're always making stupid comments about him when we see him. Mom met him. Mom knows him. He's always telling her about running, trying to get her to go out to the track and stuff like that."

"Oh," I said. "Great."

"She doesn't like him either," Rachel said. "She thinks he's a drip. But he's always real nice to me. He showed me some stuff on Richie's Apple one day when Richie wasn't there. I don't think he's a drip, really."

"Well, if you don't think so I guess he's not." I swerved to miss a dog that was ambling across the road, nose to the concrete. "But he shouldn't hold his breath about getting Theo out to the track."

"Mom isn't the type, right?"

"That's it," I said. "At least she wasn't."

"He calls me Peaches, sometimes. That's pretty drippy."

"Yep," I said.

"Peaches," she said, repeating the word with real distaste. "Outside of that he's all right."

"Good," I said, nodding.

"Dad?" Rachel said. "I mean, is Mom taking out her frustrations on that hole or something?"

I spun the steering wheel to the right, bumping the car over the edge of the curb outside Long John Silver's. "No. She'll probably end up planting a bush. You know how she is. She doesn't know what she wants to do, but she knows she wants to do something, so she just starts. Later she'll figure out how to use it." I stopped short of the only available parking space. "Does this place have a drive-through? I don't remember."

"No," Rachel said. "Go on, park."

After we ordered we sat at a wood plank table next to an olive trash barrel that was lined with a creamy tan plastic bag. Both Rachel and I made faces at the barrel. She said, "So why don't you help her? Why don't you get a shovel and help her?"

"I offered," I said. "She turned me down flat." I grabbed Rachel's shoulder and squinted at her. "You're worrying too much, Kid. You got to take it easy here."

"I think she's been acting funny ever since we bought that house. I wish we were back at the apartment."

A pretty college-age girl in a small blue halter and white shorts dumped a plateful of half-eaten fried food into the barrel and then smiled at us. "Sorry about this mess," she said, indicating the trash. "I couldn't do it."

I smiled at her.

She banged her tray on the edge of the trashcan, then rubbed her stomach with her free hand. "I feel like I'm sorry I'm alive."

"That bad, huh?" I said.

"Talking sludge," she said. "I'd hate to see the inside of me right about now."

Rachel said, under her breath, "Same here."

I gave her a nasty look and said, to the girl, "It's usually all right, isn't it? Or do you always hate it after you've done it?"

"She can't hate it that much," Rachel said.

This time I knew the girl heard her. I stuck out my hands in a shrug and looked at Rachel. "Hey. What's going on? Settle down, will you?"

"I can take care of myself," Rachel said.

The girl kept rubbing her bare stomach, more to aggravate Rachel than to interest me, I guessed. "Go easy, O.K.? How old are you?"

"Thirteen," Rachel said. "And he's my father." She rammed her forefinger into my arm a couple of times.

"Nice to meet you," the girl said. She put a foot up on the seat of the adjacent table and started tying new knots in the laces of her running shoes. "My name's Kelsey." She finished the first shoe and started the second. "I didn't mean to be tasteless and mess up your dinner. I'm sorry."

I waved at her. "Don't worry."

"It's O.K.," Rachel said. "I'm sorry, too."

I said, "This is Rachel and I'm Henry. The thing is, we've already ordered about a hundred pounds of fish. We're locked in, so to speak."

"It isn't that bad. I guess I was just trying to be interesting or something. Some of it is pretty good, really. The fries are terrific."

"We've had it before," Rachel said.

"I'm being silly, probably. I just want to get out of town, go to the beach, but it's hard to tell this time of year—it's getting cool at night and sometimes, at the beach, it's real cold this late. I could take a sweater, I guess."

"Sure," I said. "Sounds like fun."

"I hope the porpoises are still moving. This time of year they usually are and they're so pretty."

"I like the pelicans," Rachel said, drawing a bird shape on the table top. She turned around and looked sideways at Kelsey. "We went to this place one time and we spent the whole time watching pelicans. They're real big."

"I know," Kelsey said. "I used to own one. No kidding. This friend of mine worked for the National Wildlife Association, and he got me this hurt pelican one time. No kidding. It couldn't fly or anything or it would've flown away, probably. I called it Rhino, because of the color, you know?"

"Brown," Rachel said.

"Right, right. I really loved Rhino a lot. He was crazy. He couldn't even stand up right. Whenever he tried to walk or anything, flap his wings, eat a fish—I got him fresh fish from the market all the time—whenever he tried to do anything he'd topple over and land on his head. He was a mess."

"You really kept a pelican as a pet?" I said.

"That's what she said," Rachel said.

"Yep," Kelsey said. "Roger—that's my friend from the National Wildlife thing—Roger and some friend of his put this cast on Rhino's wing, but Rhino kept bashing the wing against things, against the lamp, table legs, walls, so finally Roger had to take him away. He told me that they had to put Rhino to sleep. I thought that was terrible."

Rachel tugged at my arm and pointed toward the cash register, where a guy in a tall white hat was waving a large sack. "It's our food. We have to go now."

Kelsey said, "Don't let it get cold whatever you do."

I got up and reached to shake hands with her. "It was nice talking to you. Hope you get to the beach."

"Yeah. Me too." She took my hand. "I didn't mean to talk your ears off. I guess I'm a little bit lonely. I'm new here. At the university. I'm from Florida, originally. St. Petersburg."

"I've been there," I said. "It's great. My wife works at the university, Conferences and Workshops."

"No kidding?"

"Yeah," Rachel said. "And right now she's out in the backyard digging a hole and waiting on this fish."

"A hole?" Kelsey looked puzzled. I wagged my hand at her and shook my head. She got the message. "I think I'm majoring in drama. That or business. I'm not sure yet. I should be sure, I mean, since I'm a junior, but I'm not. I was at this party school in Florida until they booted me."

She walked with us to the counter, her hands stuck in the pockets of her shorts. I paid nine dollars and forty cents for our food, then followed Rachel outside. "Well," I said, when the three of us got to the car. I looked at the sky for a second. "Well, I hope you get it figured out. It's a hard choice—business or drama. I don't know what I'd do."

"Oh, I'll make it," Kelsey said. "I'm leaning toward business. More practical, you know? Doesn't make any sense to risk it all on one throw."

"That's true enough," I said.

"If you hit, you hit, though," she said. "There's that to think about." She stepped closer to me to let a family in a Pontiac get into the parking place next to mine. Then she patted Rachel's head. "O.K., well, I'll go on, I guess. Maybe I'll meet your mother at school. Maybe I'll give her a picture of Rhino for you—you want a picture of Rhino?"

"Sure," Rachel said. She opened the car door and slid across the seat. "Thanks. That'd be great."

G OING HOME I drove through River Bottom, a land development project for which I'd done the graphics. Rachel complained that the fish would get cold, but I said it wasn't that far out of the way. "They look terrific, Dad," she said, when I showed her the first two signs.

A dozen houses in the development were already occupied. All but one had power boats in the driveways. There weren't any trees, just saplings with black hose collars and wires tethering them to the ground. Some dogs ran around in the street smelling the concrete.

Rachel said, "How much are these places?"

"Eighty thousand," I said. "They look as if they're selling pretty well."

"I like the ones that aren't built yet," she said. "Like that one." She pointed out the window at a house that was stud walls and rafters, no siding or roof. "I like them when you can still see through them."

I turned on Beverly Jane Lane, a cul-de-sac named after the developer's wife. "I want to go by the office and see this site plan. Then we can go."

"Sure," she said. She had her palms flat on either side of her on the blue vinyl seat. "Dad? Did you like that girl?"

"I don't know," I said. "Why?"

"Just wondering." She made her hands into claws and crawled them forward over the front of the seat cushion and down toward the floor. "She was pretty, wasn't she?"

"Pretty pretty," I said.

"Big," Rachel said, crawling her hands back up onto the seat. "You know what I want more than anything else in the world? I want to be tall. Seven feet tall. Eight feet. Have you ever seen a girl eight feet tall?"

"Nope." I passed the office and decided not to stop.

"An eight-foot-tall girl would be great. A real tower of power." She was quiet for a minute, then shook her head and made a retching sound. "Richie Farmer has bad breath. He smells like butter all the time. He gets so close to your face when he's talking, too. I just tell him. I just point at it." She made the sound again. "Are we going home yet?"

"On our way," I said.

On the access road there was a dark-green Volvo behind us, keeping its distance. At the stoplight the car pulled up in the next lane. It was Kelsey. She tapped her horn and waved. We waved back. She went one way and we went the other, but then she kept appearing as we drove back to the house. Rachel said, "She's following us, Dad. Look. There she is again." We were at an intersection waiting for a light. The Volvo was peeking out from behind a wiener-shaped restaurant sign.

"I don't like it," I said.

Rachel slugged me in the arm and gave me her how-dumb-can-you-get look. "Sure, Dad. You really hate it a lot."

"Are you sure that's her? What is she doing?"

"I don't know," Rachel said, twisting in the seat to look out the back window as we went through the intersection. "Maybe she wants to see where we go."

I took a detour through a car dealership and went down an alley that let out into the empty parking lot of a shopping center. I crossed the lot, dodging lampposts and broken glass, and came out on a street that ran parallel to Palm, about three blocks away.

"That was swift," Rachel said. "Why don't we just shoot up some rockets?"

A few seconds after we pulled into the driveway, Kelsey pulled in behind us. "Hi again," she said, jumping out of her car. "I followed you, did you notice?"

"We noticed," Rachel said. "You scared Dad."

"Oh. I'm sorry." Kelsey was nervous. She fiddled with her hands, folding the fingers on one hand in and out of the fingers of the other, and she twisted back and forth on her feet, first on one, then the other. Standing on our front lawn she seemed less sure of herself than at the restaurant.

"Why not come on in?" I said, pointing the white sack toward the front door.

"Sure," Rachel said. "If we don't like the fish we can always bury it."

"Thanks. What do you mean bury? Is that a joke, I guess?"

Rachel linked arms with Kelsey and started her toward the front of the house. "The hole. I told you about the hole Mom's digging, didn't I?"

Across the street, Armstrong and his mother were sitting in the driveway, cross-legged, facing each other. It looked as if they were playing some kind of card game. Armstrong yelled, "Yo! Hey!"

I turned and waved the sack in his direction.

"Got one?" he yelled.

I shook my head and waved again, then wrapped an arm around Kelsey's shoulder. "Let's get inside."

"That's our weird neighbor," Rachel said, explaining to Kelsey why we were almost running up the porch steps. "Sometimes he asks me to come over and stuff, you know the kind."

"Boy, do I," Kelsey said. When we were inside she turned to look across at Armstrong. "They used to do that to me all the time. One old guy who was a friend of my father's used to make me take his blood pressure all the time. I was a nurse's aide when I started high school, you know? So this guy had seen me in my uniform and everything, and— oh, you know."

"Yuck," Rachel said.

"Yeah," Kelsey said. "He made me do it on his thigh because he said that was the only way to get a really good reading."

Theo was sitting at the kitchen table, her arms covered with mud. "I watered it down," she said. "To loosen things. You've been gone a long time, haven't you?"

"This is Kelsey," Rachel said. "She's at your school. She wanted to meet you."

"Hi," Kelsey said.

"Hello," Theo said. "Sorry I'm so messy. I've been in the yard all day."

Kelsey folded her arms across her chest and grinned. "It's fun, isn't it? I used to do that back home."

I opened the bag and started pulling out the individually wrapped orders of fish. "Get some plates, will you, Rachel?" I said.

"I'm going to take Kelsey to my room to clean up," Rachel said. "O.K.? Then I'll get the plates."

"Go on," Theo said. "I'll do the table. Just give me a second to wash my hands."

"I'll do it," I said. "Rachel, do you want milk?"

"You don't drink milk with fish, Dad," she said. "You're so out of it sometimes. C'mon, Kelsey."

Theo watched Rachel and Kelsey go, then got up and rinsed her hands and forearms in the sink, then dried them on a pink paper towel. She said, "I really wish you wouldn't buy these pink towels. I hate pink."

"She followed us home," I said, pulling dishes out of the cabinet. "I think she's kind of crazy or something, I don't know. Where's Harold?"

"Looks scared," Theo said. "Set five, will you? Clare called. She's on her way."

I took another plate off the shelf.

"You know what, Henry? Holes are interesting. I love it when they're building a big building or something and they have to dig this giant hole first. They're so beautiful."

"Uh-huh," I said.

"Do you know what I'm talking about?" She pushed an open hand back over her head, combing the hair back, leaving some stray hairs in an off-center peak.

"Yes, I do," I said.

"I wish we were having pork chops," Theo said. "I'd love a pork chop tonight."

I put five plates around the kitchen table. Theo sat down and started passing out the silverware. Her fingernails looked like black moons.

"Maybe we could make it into a pool," I said. "Over time. Dig out the whole yard and make a pool. What do you think?"

"Maybe it wasn't such a great idea," she said.

"No, I mean it. Now that we've got the house we might as well do the whole thing."

"Don't rub it in, O.K.?" Theo took off her thin silver necklace and twisted it around her fingers until the tips of the digits turned purple, then she unwound the chain and twisted it again, on different fingers. "I don't feel good, Henry. I feel lousy. Please don't talk swimming pools, O.K.?" She pushed her chair away from the table, put her plate back into the cabinet, and left, quietly shutting the bedroom door behind her.

I stayed in the kitchen. In Rachel's room, Rachel and Kelsey were trying to outdo each other with animal noises.

After Theo and Rachel left Monday morning I decided I didn't want to work, so I went back to bed and tried to sleep. I'd been up until three-thirty watching *The Swinging Cheerleaders* on Cinemax. In the morning I got a forty-five-minute nap. When I woke up the second time I felt worse, so I sat on the edge of the bed for a while, hoping my head would clear. I was still waiting when Cindy called. "I think I'd better come talk to you," she said. "Are you ready?"

"I'm in bed," I said.

"All the better. I'll give you a couple of minutes if you insist."

"Can't you just tell me on the phone?"

"Have you looked at it? The hole? Since yesterday?"

"No. We had company. I didn't go outside."

"Look at it, O.K.? I'll be over in a minute."

She hung up. I got out of bed and went to the back window to see what she was talking about. The hole was bigger than I'd expected—about seven feet in diameter. Harold was sniffing around the edge, his tail up and wagging thoughtfully. I got dressed and waited for the doorbell.

Cindy was wearing a black denim jumpsuit that looked brand-new. "I'm reading this as a metaphor," she said, after I'd opened the door. "I mean, I talked to her, but what she said wasn't anything—you see what I'm getting at? She likes holes and all that. So I figure it's a metaphor for trouble."

"Trouble?" I said, backing into the kitchen.

"Don't ask," she said. "A metaphor works in many ways to release the feelings of an individual. Let me explain this, O.K.? Metaphor is very complex. Take my field. Architecture. In architecture everything is metaphor. Take Paris, for example."

"Paris," I said. "Never been there."

"If ever a city was a woman, it's Paris. This great gash of a river through there, through the center. Banks rising up on each side—get it? And what do you think is over there on the side? Huh?"

"I give up." I was looking in the cabinet where the dishes were. There weren't many clean dishes.

"Eiffel Tower," she said. "Metaphor locates people's central concerns, lets a person express things that a person otherwise is unable to express. So that's what clued me in."

I handed her a red mug of coffee and pointed to the sugar bowl which was open on the kitchen table.

"Thanks," she said, waving off the sugar and shaking her

head. "I'm thinking Theo is depressed. The digging is a model of the emotional digging that's going on. I mean, she's digging around in herself trying to find out why she's so depressed."

"I see what you mean," I said. I drew a couple of plump cows on the pink message pad that was on the table.

"Part of it is the house. You hate it. You don't want to be here. Everything was fine until you got this house."

"Wrong," I said.

"Everything wasn't fine? What are you saying?"

I smiled and stared at her and didn't answer.

"O.K. Don't tell me. Maybe she hates the house. The house figures in it some way or other, I got that very strongly from our conversation. And there's the Clare business."

"Not my idea."

"I don't mean you and Clare. Clare hates you. I mean, she doesn't hate you, but she sure doesn't like you. But Theo wants to be like her, more or less."

"Oh." I tried to draw an alligator, but it didn't come out so well, so I turned it into a barbell. "I'm looking forward to that."

"In part, in part," Cindy said. "The point is she's digging this hole and it's a signal, a drawing of your attention to an area of interpersonal conflict. You need to go with it. Get out there and dig. Show her you're interested in her depression. Be careful, though—you don't want to take over."

Harold came to the back door and pawed the screen, so I got up and let him in. He went directly to Cindy and started smelling her feet. "Harold," I said.

"If he messes with me he's fertilizer," she said.

"Don't worry." I slapped my thigh. "Harold. Move. Hey, Harold." He didn't move, so I grabbed him by the collar and dragged him into the bedroom.

"Maybe you should get Theo back into school," Cindy said, when I returned. "She gets a free course, right?"

"You want more coffee?"

"No. I've got to go. I just wanted to give you my read on this hole." She wiped lipstick off the rim of the mug. "Who was the girl in the Volvo?"

"She's a new friend for Rachel, from the school, the university. A natural babysitter."

"She didn't look like a babysitter to me." Cindy pushed away from the table. She crossed the kitchen to the back door and looked out into the yard. "Theo like her?"

"I don't think Theo noticed she was here."

"I'll bet she didn't." Cindy turned and glanced around the kitchen. "Maybe you should do something interesting in here. Surprise her. Kind of a call-and-response thing, you know? What about that?"

Theo had forgotten the hole by the time she came home. She was early and she brought the movie *Blade Runner*, which she'd borrowed from the video club at the university. Rachel stayed at school for a meeting, then went to Richie's house to study, so Theo made us sandwiches and we watched this movie, which she said had fabulous art direction, set decoration, cinematography, and special effects. Clare had suggested it, she told me.

When the movie was over she said, "I want to make love now. What about you?"

"Sure," I said. That didn't sound right, so I reached over and said, "Yes. Please," touching the back of her neck with my fingernails.

She got off the couch. "It's a bad idea, I know. But maybe it would help." She looked out the front window at Armstrong's house and then, without turning, said, "No. I guess not. Never mind."

"Wait a minute," I said.

"I guess we could go out and dump all the dirt back in that hole. I don't know what I was doing."

I stood beside her at the window. I could see the silhouettes of Armstrong and his mother on the curtains in the corner room across the street. "Cindy says you think I don't like the house."

"I don't know about you, but I hate it. I feel alone here. I wish we'd taken one of those things where Jerry and Grace live—what's it called?"

"Madeline Place."

"I like people around all the time. Like where Clare lives with Joel. Where you and she were. I'd like to live there." She sighed and riffled her hair with her fingers. "I don't want to mess with dirt tonight, O.K.? I'm too tired. But it's supposed to rain. I heard it on the radio coming home.

"The rain won't hurt anything. Besides, me and Harold love it."

She put her arm around my waist and leaned against my shoulder. "Yes?"

"Pretty much," I said.

"She gave me a talk yesterday in the yard. Told me what it meant, me digging like that. But she doesn't believe it. She just wants something to talk about. I don't think Duncan ever talks to her. I don't know what they do in there at night. Have you noticed that the lights go out at eight o'clock? He goes around and turns off all the lights except the light in the den and the one in the kitchen. She told me he sits in the den and reads magazines all night, and he makes her use the earphones if she wants to watch television. She goes to bed instead."

"Fun. Maybe she should dig a hole the size of an ark in the backyard. Get his attention."

We went into the kitchen side by side, our arms bumping against each other. "Not funny," she said. "I want something chocolate. I wonder what happened to Clare. Has she called or anything?"

"I haven't seen her since last night. I think she's avoiding me. She probably left while I was taking my morning nap."

We looked for chocolate but couldn't find any. Theo took a blackened banana from the bowl alongside the toaster. I washed my hands. She leaned on the counter and ate, watching her reflection in the kitchen window. "I guess I ought to call Joel's and see what's happening. See if he mulched her."

Rachel called at ten and asked if she could stay the night at Kelsey's. We were in bed. "I don't know," I said. "Ask your mother." I handed the phone to Theo and crawled under the cord so I could get to the bathroom. The rain Theo predicted had started. It was coming hard, blanketing the house with a steady noise. I heard part of Theo's conversation. Kelsey had gotten Rachel at school and gone with her to Richie's. I went back to the bedroom with a white towel over my shoulder.

"What's the decision?" I asked.

"I let her stay, but I don't know if I should have. This girl Kelsey, isn't she too old for Rachel? She apparently lives right over here." Theo waved her hand above her head. "Those apartments on Slide Street, you know, the new ones."

I nodded and wiped my face on a corner of the towel.

"I got the number if we want to change our minds," Theo said.

I picked up the blue towel that I'd been using to cover my eyes in the morning and took it into the bathroom to the dirty-clothes hamper. "If you're worried I'll get her."

"I want to go out in the rain. Do you?"

"Now? I hadn't thought about it." I sat down at the end of the bed and started arranging my towel.

"I want to. Will you come with me?" She pushed at me with her feet. "Will you?" She looked young. I said I'd go, thinking she wouldn't want to if I agreed. I was wrong. She rolled out of bed and dragged me through the house and out to the back porch. We stood there hand in hand for a few minutes, watching the rain. In the yellow porch light I could see the hole, half full of water, a few leaves floating on its surface. Rain scented the air. Flowers too—camelias, I think, from the Browns' yard. Theo went down the two steps into the yard, then walked circles around the hole.

"You promised," she said, stopping to call me out into the rain. "Come on."

The rain was startling and cold at first, but after a minute I was used to it. Theo sat at the edge of the hole and dropped her legs over the edge, dangling her feet into the clay-colored water. "It's not much, is it?" she said. "This water down here is warm, though." She splashed the water with her feet. Her nightgown, which was cotton, like a man's shirt, was already soaked at the bottom and spotted above with muddy circles.

Harold peeked from under the house, yawned so hard that he wheezed, then crawled out and wandered over to where we were. Theo wrapped an arm around his neck and hugged him. He pulled back out of her headlock and then shook himself vigorously, spraying us with the water from his coat.

"You're pretty good at this, aren't you," I said to the dog. When I reached out to pat his rump he turned around and looked at my hand, then up at me.

"It's O.K., Harold," Theo said. She wrestled his head back under her arm. "He's a friend."

She stepped down into the hole. The water was knee deep, dragging the hem of her nightgown back and forth. "You're getting all the way in?" I said.

"You too. And Harold." She grabbed his collar and pulled him to the edge of the hole, talking to him. He straightened his front legs, but finally they buckled and he half slid and half jumped into the hole. When he was in she dropped to her knees. "Your turn, Henry."

"What about pneumonia?" I squatted at the edge of the hole. "Theo? You ready to go in and go to bed?"

"In a minute. You have to get in here first." She had both arms around Harold, keeping him in the hole. A light went on at the back of the Browns' house, then it went off again.

I got in. She splashed the water, slapping at it with the palm of her hand. Harold barked and bounced up and down, which splashed more water. Theo was laughing and having a good time. She tackled me around the knees and knocked me down in the hole and then, when we were both sitting in it, she wiped at her hair, pushing it back off her forehead, and began to sing "The Battle Hymn of the Republic," beating time on the water. After a minute I sang, too. We held hands and rocked back and forth, singing, Harold prancing around us, in and out of the hole like some dervish, and then I asked her to sing this cowboy song that doesn't have any words, a kind of yodeling song she used to do when we were out driving on the highway—I told her it sounded like "Bali High," so it took her a while to remember—but then she got it and we did ten minutes of that before the three of us went inside and straight into the shower.

J OEL CAUGHT me coming home from work a few days after Clare told him she wasn't moving back to his apartment, she was staying with us until further notice. It was drizzling, and the streets were slick, the lawns sodden, bordered with curbside sleeves of water. The afternoon was dark, supple, tree limbs so thoroughly soaked they arched like ropes toward the grass. Everywhere there was the sound of water rushing, or falling, or dripping. Or being fizzed up by car tires, or whisked away by the constant clapping wipers. Joel drove by me about six blocks from the house. I recognized his car and guessed he was coming to get Clare. When he went by, I waved. Then he got in front and hit the brakes hard. I swerved to avoid smashing into him and jumped the curb.

He got out and walked slowly back to my car. He looked mad. His face was red. I rolled down the window. "What are you doing?"

"Get out," he said, grabbing the door handle. The door was locked, so it didn't open.

"What's the problem?" I opened the door and bumped him with it, then closed it again. "Sorry. Didn't mean to hit you."

"No. You just want my woman."

I was glad he was direct. I shook my head. "You got the wrong guy, Bucko. I used to be married to her. She's Theo's friend now."

"I'm gonna marry your face," he said. "Get out here."

I crooked my elbow back and up and snapped down the door lock, then rolled up the window about halfway. "Take it easy," I said.

He hit the roof of my car with his palm. "Take it easy," he said, whining at me. "Jesus, I hate you guys." He swung around in the street, both his hands fists. "Tell her to get out of your house, why don't you? Shit." He leaned on the car, his face close to the window. "What are you, some kind of liberal, or what?"

I shook my head. "She wants to stay. What do you want me to do?"

"You can give a guy a break. Jesus, don't be such a weenie."

"I should tell her how nice you are, is that it?"

He snorted. "That's cute, Henry. That's a cute little piece of business. That makes me feel just fine." He thumped his stiff second finger into his chest. "I just wanted to talk to you before you got to the house. I need to talk to somebody." He shook his head and whistled, then pointed toward the passenger seat of my car. "Let me get in here and talk to you a minute."

I leaned forward and pressed my forehead against the top of the steering wheel. "I don't have anything to say. Clare has decided—she's only been there a couple of weeks, and she's out more than she's in anyway. What's the big deal?"

"Come on, Henry." He started around the car and said something I couldn't hear, then wagged his hand to tell me to unlock the door.

Cars were going by. Instead of doing what Joel wanted I pulled my door handle and got out to see if I was going to have trouble getting off the curb. My front wheels were up in somebody's lawn, but, apart from that, there wasn't any problem.

He stayed on his side of the car. "I need a little help, Henry," he said.

"I don't think I'm your man—I couldn't even stay married to her a year. She left me for a jeweler, remember?" The rain was harder, heavier. I got back in the car and opened his door.

"I'm sorry about the brakes business," he said. "That was

stupid. I don't know what I was doing. I wouldn't have hit you, though. I can't hit people. When I was a kid I was always getting beat up because I couldn't hit anybody. It was awful." He was looking out the windshield toward a yellow brick house that had a handmade sign, SAM IS SICK, tacked to the side door. Joel wiped his head with his palm, pushing the hair forward. "I like you, Henry."

"She won't be there forever," I said. "Besides, you're with her most of the time anyway."

"I'm trying. I think I'm going to buy this house. You know the house?"

"She told us. I think you should take it."

"I've got six months on my lease. Nassar asks about you all the time. He wants to know about Theo. Listen, do you think seventy grand is good for this house?"

"It's about right."

"I don't have any friends," he said. He swept his hand across the dashboard of my car and then looked at the dust on his fingers. "Maybe that's a bad thing."

"Why don't we have some dinner?"

"You mean at your house?"

"Sure. Watch some TV, beat up the women—how's that sound?"

He looked at me quickly, squinting, then looked back out the windshield. "Clare tell you that?"

"I wasn't thinking. It was a joke. Stupid."

"Did she tell you about holding her sister's twenty-two on me? Or the time she cut my ankles with the peeler?" He yanked on the door handle and pushed the car door open with his foot. "I haven't hit her in a year. I go outside. I tell her to stay the hell away from me and then I go sit in the parking lot. She watches me from the window, I've seen her peeking around the shade. Sometimes I just sit there and laugh it's so pathetic." He got out and gave me signals about which way to turn the wheels to get off the curb. When I was back in the street he said, "I have to stop at the store first." Then he waved me by.

* * *

Nobody was at the house when I got there. There was a message from Theo on the note pad: "Gone to Colorado." I got two cans of beer, one for Joel, then tore the note off the pad, said, "Me, I went to Pluto," out loud to nobody, and went out to the front of the house, wondering if he'd come and I hadn't heard him. He wasn't there. Armstrong pulled his bicycle out his side door, into the rain. He was done up in a canary-yellow sweat suit with maroon stripes from the ankles to the armpits. He was very careful coming out of his house and down the concrete steps. Once the bike was on the ground, he went back and locked the door, then stopped on the landing to adjust the zipper of his sweat jacket. He rolled the bicycle down the driveway to the street, pushed off the curb, and got up into the saddle. He must've seen me on the porch. He turned and stared right at me, then twisted the handlebars and rode up my drive and onto the grass. "I figure we ought to meet sooner or later," he said, getting off the bike. "My name's Armstrong. I live over here." He pointed to his house. "Lived there when I was a kid and live there now. What's your name?"

I had opened the screen door when he started into my driveway, but I didn't go outside. "Henry," I said. "You want to get in out of this mess?" I pushed the door open wider.

He grinned, showing me a row of dark-yellow teeth. He was wearing a red baseball hat that had a little four-inch arm connected to the bill, hanging down alongside his glasses. "Can't hurt. Got to get Alma inside, though, if you don't mind." He patted the handlebar, which had a bell mounted near the right grip.

"Bring her in." I waved toward the porch. "Plenty of room."

It was the first time I'd seen him up close. He was past fifty, knobby-looking, with hollow cheeks and splotchy skin. He looked like a drinker. The gadget attached to his hat was a tiny rearview mirror. When the bike was inside and up on its kickstand he turned around and stuck out his hand. "Andrew Armstrong. I live over there with my mother, Adele."

"Pleased to meet you," I said. We shook hands. He was wearing several rings, big, lumpy things—one was turquoise, one a round-topped purple stone I didn't recognize.

"So," he said. He held on to my hand as he looked around. "This is the porch, huh?"

"Yep," I said.

"Uh-huh. Been a long time. Haven't been in this place since I was a kid. That boy that was here before you sure worked on it all the time. Doesn't look like he got a whole lot done, though, does it?" He went to one of the windows between the living room and the porch, and peered inside. "So. That's his famous fireplace, huh?"

"That's it. Do you want to take a look? I'll get you a beer." I raised my can in his direction and shoved open the door into the house.

"I'm on the wet side." He tapped his feet, one after the other, on the gray porch floorboards. "Where're those women?"

"Not here," I said. "Don't worry about the shoes." I motioned for him to follow me into the house.

He came to the door but stopped before he was inside. "I don't know. I feel like I'm walking on sponges."

"Take them off if you want to."

"Got no socks." He made a face at me, a clownish, awkward smile and widened eyes. "Don't like socks. Never have, never will. They're too small. Too tight. Strangle the feet. Socks turn 'em white and get these red marks all over 'em. No sir."

"Sounds like a problem. Why don't you come in and I'll get us another beer." I tinkled the last drops of beer in the can I was holding.

"The other woman gone, too?"

"Gone too," I said.

"Ah." He stepped over the threshold. "Nobody home but us chickens."

"That's it. Let me get the beer. Do you want a glass?"

"Can's fine," he said. "Can's O.K. by me anytime."

I got the beer I'd opened for Joel and a fresh can from the refrigerator and went back to the living room. Armstrong was squatting by the front window, staring outside toward his house.

"I'm sorry we haven't had a chance to talk before this," I said, sitting on the couch and putting his beer on the coffee table alongside a stack of magazines. "We've been moving in, trying to get the place set up. You know how that is."

"Oh, I don't miss everything. Ought to get you some better drapes along here, though. Come night you can see right in." He swiveled around on the ball of his foot, the shoe squeaking on the hardwood, and made a swimming-fish gesture with his hand. "Right in. That my beer?"

I nodded. "We're going to take care of it. I think she wants some special thing, for the windows, I mean. She may have already ordered something, as a matter of fact."

"Uh-huh, uh-huh." His knee bones popped loudly as he straightened up. "I know what you mean on that ordering business. We used to order all our clothes, Adele and me, from this outfit in Boston, but things got lost, took a long time, they sent the wrong stuff half the time—ordering is trouble. I stay away from ordering." He picked up his beer and took it to the hall doorway, looked back into that part of the house. "Your wife the one with the blond hair or the other one?" he asked.

"The other one."

"Yeah. I like her better," he said. He gave me a thumbs-up sign. "The blond-haired one your sister or something? Wife's sister?"

"She's just visiting," I said. "My ex-wife. She's having some trouble with her husband, and, you know, we're friends, she and Theo are old friends, so she's bunking in for a couple of weeks."

"Been here near a couple of weeks already, as I figure it. Her husband the rotater in the silver Torino?"

"Yep. Joel. He's supposed to be here now. I saw him on my way home." I went to the window and looked out.

"Probably got held up," Armstrong said. "What about the girl? She from the first or second? Or is she visiting, too? This her room right here?"

I followed him into Rachel's room. "She's Theo's," I said. "From a first marriage."

"Uh-huh. She's cute." He went to the window in the front corner of her bedroom and looked out, then turned around and looked toward her closet as if checking a sight line. "How old is she, fifteen? Twelve?"

"Thirteen," I said. "Just had a birthday."

"And the other girl? What's she?"

"You mean Kelsey? About twenty, blond?" I held my hand up at about Kelsey's height.

"That'd be it," he said.

"Just a friend. Rachel's. You want to see the rest of the house?"

He stopped and smoothed the spread at the foot of Rachel's bed. "I don't guess I need to see it. I been out awhile and Adele's over there watching TV. I can't stay out too long or she'll call up the police. She's old, and your old people have a tendency to get a little nervous, but I like her anyway. She's not a young thing anymore, though. Gets nervous real easy. I take care of her. We get along fine." He came back out into the hallway and peeked at the kitchen, the back bedroom, Clare's room, then went into the living room. "I thought I remembered the three bedrooms from when old Mrs. Kroner was here. It's an awful small house to be having three bedrooms."

"Mrs. Kroner was the original owner, right?"

"Yeah. Mrs. Kroner was here when I was a boy. I used

to come over all the time. I guess she was a decent sort, in spite of everything. What are you, about thirty-five? Thirty-six?"

"About that." I smiled at him. "But I'm moving fast."

"Sure you are. That's right." He pulled a red washcloth out of one of the pockets of his sweat suit and took off his hat, wiped his forehead, then wrapped the cloth over his first finger and started cleaning the mirror attached to the hat. "Goes fast for a bit, but it slows down. I know that."

I nodded at him and watched the hairs pop up on his scalp as he wrinkled his brow.

"Well," he said, putting the cap back on and pocketing the washcloth. "I've got to go on now. I guess I don't have to ride every day. Tell you what, though, it's good for you. I've had this bicycle since nineteen fifty-eight, and I feel a lot better. Ought to get you one. But don't let 'em trick you into one of those thin-tire jobs. I tried one a couple of years ago. Boy." He wheezed and shook his head. "Those Italians got problems, if you get my meaning."

It was dark outside. The lights in the houses across the street were on. I went out onto the porch. "Think it'll rain?" I said, opening the screen door.

"That's mighty funny," he said. He shook my hand, adjusted his hat, and pushed the bike off its stand. "Well. I guess I'll roll her on."

By eight o'clock I wondered if Theo really had gone to Colorado. Joel never showed up, so I called him. Clare wasn't there. He was watching a National Geographic special on snakes. I told him about the note and he said, "Sounds like a joke to me. They probably went to a movie. You ought to see this show. It's incredible."

I said, "If you hear from Clare ask her to call me, will you?"

"Will do. Keep me posted," he said.

Theo called the minute I hung up the phone. "We're in

Boulder," she said. "I left. I wanted some time by myself. A week or so. Rachel's with Kelsey. Clare knows people here. You want the number?" Her voice was different. Flat, matter-of-fact. I asked where she was, but she wouldn't say, she just offered the telephone number again. "I know you're going to worry about this, Henry. But I can't talk about it now. Do you want the number or not?" She gave me the number, then said, "I've got to go. Maybe I'll call tomorrow."

After she disconnected I held on to the receiver until the dial tone came back. I listened to that for a couple of minutes, then punched the button and called Joel. I told him they were in Colorado.

"Don't be silly," he said.

When he was convinced, he wanted to come over so we could figure out what to do. "Our wives are gone," he said.

Cindy Brown called. The first thing she said was, "It's going to be all right, Henry."

"Thanks," I said.

"Rachel can stay with us. That might make her feel better. Have you heard from Theo?"

"She called," I said.

"They made it, then. That's great. I mean, that they're safe and everything. Well, Rachel can stay here, remember."

"We'll be O.K.," I said. "Thanks."

I took a Pepsi out of the refrigerator, went into the living room, and stretched out on the couch. Cindy called back in fifteen minutes. "I've been thinking. Maybe I'd better come over. It's not good to be alone at a time like this. I mean, even though it's probably nothing."

I looked at the telephone receiver, holding it away from my face. "Well, thank you," I said.

Rachel came in half an hour later. "You O.K., Dad? Mom said I should take care of you. You need anything? Dinner?"

"Not hungry." I pointed to one of the kitchen chairs.

"Let's sit here. You want to tell me what's going on?"

"I came home from school and they were all packed up, standing outside in the driveway by Clare's car. Mom said she was taking a vacation."

"That's all?"

"Yep. I came in here and found the note, then I went over there to tell them I wasn't coming, in case Mom had said I was. Then I was with Kelsey. What's the big deal? You didn't know about it?"

"Nope," I said.

Joel knocked on the kitchen door, then opened it and came in. He was carrying a white paper sack. "Barbecue. I figured we'd need it for the vigil." He patted Rachel's head. "We're talking modern women here, Kiddo. You had better listen."

"We can have an O.K. time, Dad," Rachel said. "We can go out and stuff. You want me to fix this up?" She snapped the barbecue out of Joel's hand and crossed to the counter, pulling foil-wrapped packages out of the bag. "Ouch. This stuff is hot."

Joel rubbed his palms together as if we were on a camping trip and the weather had suddenly turned cold. "First of all, I don't think they're in Colorado."

Cindy and Duncan arrived at nine-thirty. Everybody sat at the kitchen table. I leaned against the counter and looked through the door at the television. Every once in a while Duncan glanced at me and solemnly shook his head as if he understood what I was going through. "I think I'm going to call her," I finally said. I pushed off the counter and started out of the room.

Cindy grabbed my wrist. "Wait. Hold on. I think I'd let her alone tonight."

"Right," Joel said, nodding vigorously. "I'm letting Clare alone."

Duncan turned and nodded approvingly at Joel. "I agree. I think we've got a handle on this one now, let's just let it slide for a day or two. Everybody needs privacy."

"I wish you would just shut up," Cindy said, pointing at Duncan."

"Maybe I'll just call and say good night. Something like that."

"Sure," Cindy said. "I'm telling you that would be the worst thing in the world you could do right now. Women don't like to be begged."

"That's right," Rachel said. "I read that in a magazine."

"You're too young to be reading that in a magazine," Cindy said. "Whatever it is."

"*Teen Beat*," Rachel said. "It was an interview with Grace Jones or somebody."

"Who's Grace Jones?" Duncan said.

"Never mind," Cindy said. She tightened her grip on my arm. "Take my word for it. Just sit tight, play it close, and everything will work out fine. If you go calling her up every five minutes you're going to spook her. It's like a cop reading you your rights."

"I'd like to read her her rights," Joel said. "Clare, I mean."

I took Cindy's advice and stayed away from the phone. After everyone left I watched TV with Rachel until she fell asleep on the floor twenty minutes into a movie about women weight lifters. I woke her up and walked her into the bedroom. She gave me a hug. "I don't think it's curtains for you, Dad."

"Thanks, Butch." I crossed the room and checked the window to be sure the drapes were shut. "I think she just got fed up."

"With what?"

I sat down on the end of Rachel's bed and picked at a stray piece of leather on the sole of one of my shoes. "Don't know. Me, I guess." I stared at my shoe for a second, then turned around and raised an eyebrow at Rachel. "On the other hand, maybe it's you."

"Dad," she said. "Your back. You look like a humpback."

"Hunch," I said, straightening my shoulders. "Not hump, hunch."

"She's probably just messing around, don't you think? Mom's sort of a flake."

"I'll tell her you said so. Who's driving tomorrow?"

"Mrs. Prable. Cindy is going to drive when it's our turn. She told me this afternoon."

"I'll drive," I said. "I can drive."

"You don't like to drive, I thought. You should hear her when she drives. She talks the whole time in this icky way. It's disgusting. She's a real porker."

I kissed Rachel and said good night, then went through the house checking the door locks. After that I cleaned up the kitchen, turned out the lights, and went back to the bedroom. The bed was made. I called Theo. Somebody named Rex had to go find her for me and then, after he'd done that, he came back to the phone to say she was coming. "One thing I want to tell you, Hank," he said. "She's fine. She looks very fine. She's just taking it easy. She and Clare are going to have a swim tomorrow, something like that. Maybe do some shopping. I don't want you to worry."

"Thanks, Rex."

"She's O.K. She really is. I mean it. She's in good hands."

When Theo got on the phone I said I was sorry to bother her so late, but I thought I ought to find out what was going on.

"I don't know," she said. "Nothing. You should see this place, Henry. It's lovely. Have you ever been to Colorado?"

I said I hadn't and asked if she was having a good time. She said she thought she was. After that we hung up.

The house was quiet. I bunched the pillows behind me, turned on the lights, and sat up in bed. I heard an airplane fly over, a small airplane. It reminded me of hot summers in Texas in the fifties, of afternoons cut by the drone of engines and the sight of tiny planes high in the blue sky. I listened hard, the way you listen to a sound that might be somebody breaking in, sat still while the plane buzzed overhead, and remembered myself, a child of ten or twelve, towheaded, wearing hand-me-down khakis and a short-sleeve seersucker shirt, probably blue, on the terrace of my father's house, staring at the sky, my hand above my eyes for shade. I remembered the backyard, large and long and bordered at the far end with a twist of bushes and trees, remembered the redwood-and-glass wall of our industrial-looking house and the milky net awnings my father had strung over the terrace—the material was translucent plastic, laminated on a grid of string, perhaps wire, stretched and secured on four-by-eights that framed the terrace. It was a bad choice for a roof, but it was hopeful.

What I thought, as I listened to the airplane's engine grow faint, was that I didn't mind being alone. As a kid I had wanted to be up there, curving across the sky, I had wanted to smell the oil and feel the vibration and hear the wind blasting off the metal, I had wanted the cold buckle of a safety harness cutting into my stomach, but now, thirty years later, I thought how quiet the engines sounded in the bedroom, how docile, and I thought of how slowly this airplane moved away, and of its distance from the ground, and how tiny and black and mysterious it would be if I went out to find it in the night sky.

THEO WAS back from Colorado in less than a week. She came with Clare in a cab from the airport, and as soon as they were inside, Clare vanished into the bathroom. Theo seemed tired—ragged eyes, pasty cheeks, runny nose. The clothes she picked out of her suitcase looked as if they hadn't been washed. She dumped them into the machine and poured herself some red wine and asked me to sit down with her in the kitchen. I hadn't called her again. She hadn't called me. I was happy to see her, but I was nervous, I wanted to ask a lot of questions. She said there wasn't much to discuss.

"I want you to move out for a while." She was swishing her wine around in the yellow plastic tumbler. "Later, maybe we can talk. Not now. Now you can get an apartment. We're keeping the house, Clare and me and Rachel. Where is Rachel, anyway?"

I said, "A movie, I think."

Theo squeezed the bridge of her nose between her thumb and forefinger. "So—can you handle this? We thought about taking Joel's place and letting you guys stay here, but we decided that wouldn't work because of you and Joel." She polished off the wine and then I followed her into the hall outside our bedroom. The bathroom door was ajar. "Clare?" she said. "May I come in a minute?"

Clare pulled open the door and stuck her head around the edge. Her hair was wet and there were bubbles of water on her shoulder. "Sure. Is Henry coming, too?"

"I'm waiting in the bedroom."

In a few minutes Clare came out wearing Theo's lemon

silk robe. She sat down next to me on the bed. "So. How
have you been getting along?"

"Do you want to explain this?"

Clare flipped the thin fabric over her knee. "Things have
broken loose, Henry. We wait and see where they stop." I
recognized the remark. I'd heard it from her before, years
ago, over the telephone. She rubbed my knee. "Don't get
crazy. You never know, maybe it'll go your way." She got
up, drew the robe's belt into a tight knot at her waist, and
went past the bath to her room.

I watched her and waited for the door to shut. When it
did, I got up and straightened the bedspread. Theo came
out wearing a pair of underpants I'd never seen before, boxy
things with scallop-cut legs and lace trim. She pulled a shirt
of mine out of the closet. She folded the shirt and placed
it neatly on the bed, then got another shirt. She said, "I'm
helping you."

"Divorce is help?"

"Am I talking divorce? Did I say the word divorce? No.
I did not. I said I wanted the house and you can get an
apartment for a while. It's not the end of the world. It may
not last. I just want to try."

"Try? Try bowling." I got up and put both shirts back in
the closet, then rubbed my forehead. "Are there aspirin in
here?" I headed for the bathroom.

She followed me. "I like Clare. We're going to live together."

"What could be more reasonable than that?"

She was carrying a pink Brooks Brothers shirt I'd had for
years, a favorite shirt of mine and one of her least favorites.
She stopped at the bathroom door and stared in at me. "I
don't mean that way. And even if I did, what's wrong with
it?" She bundled the shirt and tossed it alongside a pile of
Clare's stuff on the bath mat.

* * *

The next night I checked into the Ramada Inn. I was in the room watching a baseball game on TBS when Joel knocked on the window with a key or something. The sound was sharp. "You scared me," I said, opening the door.

"It's time I scared somebody." He hadn't shaved and his hair was swooping around his head as if it'd been hit with a pillow a few too many times. He was wearing a Hawaiian shirt that was about a size and a half too small. He handed me a brown sack and slouched into one of the two shiny plastic-covered chairs backed up against the window. "We've done it now. I told you about this."

I squeezed the paper around the bottle, then twisted the bag to tighten it around the neck. "I'm O.K.," I said.

"Listen to the man. He's a tough guy all the sudden. He's a mean machine." He put his feet up on the end of the bed and slid farther down in the chair, hiding his eyes with his hands. "Clare got all her stuff out of the apartment. She took almost everything. Shoes—did she collect shoes when you were together? She even took the box of shoes I had at the office. She must have a hundred pair of shoes. Took every one." He got the bottle and went into the bathroom. "You want a drink?" he said, leaning out of the bathroom and holding two plastic glasses upside down on his first and second fingers.

I shook my head and stuffed an extra pillow behind my back, stretching out on the bed.

He made his drink and sat down again. "Now you see what it's like," he said.

I said, "You know, about a year ago, I went in the bathroom to get a Maalox, and I was thinking about something else, so I yanked open the drawer and this giant bug skitters around in there, making this scratchy noise, then it jumps out and hits me in the face. Ever since, when I open a drawer in the bathroom, I'm cautious. I do it slow. The thing is it doesn't apply to other drawers, in the kitchen or anywhere—I open them as if nothing ever happened."

"What's that mean?" he said.

"Means I don't see." I watched a couple of kids in striped shirts work out on the lighted jungle gym that was in the motel courtyard. I watched salesmen go back and forth across the lawn, and brightly colored families going to dinner in the blue-glassed restaurant that poked out next to the pool, and people making special trips to the desk, and a few couples out to stretch their legs after a day in the car.

Joel nursed his drink and stole glances at the television, which was still on, although I'd turned the sound off when he came in. The room was damp, felt damp. I'd set the air conditioner to maximum cool earlier, and hadn't changed the adjustment. He said, "You can stay at my place. I mean, if you want to. There may be an apartment vacant. I saw some guys moving this morning. These six kids had this one-bedroom up on top, you know? One of those that backs up on the alley."

"I may have to," I said.

"You want me to call Nassar? I can call him from here if you want. He remembers you."

"He probably remembers Clare."

"He doesn't have to remember Clare," Joel said.

"Oh, right. I wasn't thinking. You think he'll give me something for a month or so, without a lease?"

"He might," Joel said. "He's O.K. You know his wife? Mariana? She's got this gorgeous hair, red. Dark red. I think it's fake, but who cares? Her sister works here."

"Here?"

"Over here, I think," Joel said. He waved his drink over his head toward the restaurant. "She's an athlete of some kind."

"I guess I should call him."

Joel pushed himself to the front of the chair and then stood up. He was wobbly. "I'll do it," he said. "What's your number? I'll go fix it up and then I'll call you."

I gave him the number, wrote it down for him on a piece of the sack, and then, after he'd used the bathroom, I walked with him out onto the balcony in front of my room.

A chubby guy in Bermuda shorts and a terrycloth tennis hat excused himself and pushed between us carrying a beach ball that was about two feet across. He said, "Howdy, neighbors," and smiled a huge smile, then bumped me with the ball. "Sorry about that," he said. His rubber sandals slapped on the concrete as he walked away from us. Six or seven rooms down he stopped in front of a door and called out, "Marie? Marie?" He waited for someone to answer the door. "Great night," he said to us. Then the door opened, bathing him in yellow light from the room. He thrust the ball forward, and said, "Gotcha a present, Sweetie," then he looked back along the balcony at us, did a Jackie Gleason zoot-step, and tilted into the room.

"Looking good," Joel said.

Rachel and Kelsey turned the corner from the breezeway where stairs emptied onto the balcony. "Two old guys having a good time," Rachel said. "Maybe we ought to leave them alone." She did a quick about-face, tugged Kelsey's arm, and pretended to head for the stairs.

"Hi," Kelsey said. She pulled Rachel back into the light.

"Who's your friend, Rachel?" Joel said. "You bring her for me?" He clapped me on the shoulder.

"We're spying," Rachel said. She wrapped her arms around my stomach and gave me a tight hug. "Mom told me where you were, so I came to see for myself." She let go of me and pushed on the metal door to my room. "This is neat," she said.

Joel said, "I'm going. I'll call you, O.K.?" He stuck out his hand to Kelsey. "I'm Joel."

"We call him Old Joel over at our house," Rachel said from the doorway. "If you catch my drift."

"Thanks, Ace," he said, reaching past me to flick Rachel's ear with his finger.

"*De nada,*" she said.

He left, stuffing the liquor bottle in his jacket pocket. Kelsey followed Rachel into the room, and I followed Kelsey, trying to read the label on the back pocket of her jeans.

After we'd gotten drinks—Tab for me and Kelsey, Mr. Pibb for Rachel—and after the television was turned off and we were all arranged on the two beds, Rachel said, "So, what's your side of the story?"

"My side? Are there sides?"

"Come on, Dad. Mom says she's a different person when you're not around. Is that right?"

"If I'm not around I don't know, do I?"

She made a face at Kelsey. "It starts this way sometimes. He won't answer the questions. It gets better."

Kelsey was still looking at the room. She seemed particularly interested in the Japanese bird painting.

"So? What's she mean about being a different person? You guys get married after all this time and now here you are at the Holiday Inn or something—what am I supposed to make of that?" Rachel rolled onto her back and walked her feet up the headboard of the bed.

"Make it a bad week," I said.

"So how long are you staying here? Just a couple of nights or something?"

"I don't know about that, Rachel."

"Oh no," she said, looking back up over her head at Kelsey. "When he starts calling me Rachel that way it means things are pretty serious."

Kelsey smoothed Rachel's hair. "Things get serious, Hotshot. It's happened to me and I'm not even twenty."

"Yeah?" Rachel said. She twisted back onto her stomach. "What happened?"

"I'm not telling." Kelsey poked a curl off Rachel's forehead. "I'm embarrassed. He was too old."

"Was he as old as you-know-who?"

"Older."

"Older than Dad? That's horrible. Didn't he smell funny?"

"Compared to what?" Kelsey grinned at me and made a moron face. "He didn't smell like a kid, if that's what you mean."

"Maybe I'd better take a quick shower," I said.

Rachel sighed dramatically. "You probably don't notice it so much, Dad, but old people smell different. You know—older."

"Right," I said.

Kelsey said, "We're headed for the zoo. You want to come?"

"We don't care if it's open," Rachel said. "We just want to go."

"It isn't open," Kelsey said. "It's nighttime. We can walk the fence and watch. They're all crawling around and stuff. I go over there a lot at night."

"Yeah," Rachel said. "And afterwards you can buy dinner and explain about you and Mom."

I looked at the TV. The game was tied. I rolled off the bed. "I like it here, Rachel. I like the smell in this bedspread, mostly. I've fallen for the Ramada in a big way. You ever look in the corner of one of these rooms? Where the floor meets the wall? No, probably not. Just as well. But, I can handle it. It's my assignment. Theo's having a space attack, and I can help. Also, she doesn't like me too much. Which is pretty bad news, I guess." I picked up the corner of the bedspread and examined the olive-green tassels. "Lousy, in fact."

She snorted. "Come on, Dad. Get your coat or something, will you?"

We went in Kelsey's Volvo, which was brand-new. Her father was a dealer, so she got a new one every year. "Sometimes," she said, "I think maybe I ought to keep something for more than a year. But then, when it comes right down to it, I go for it." She shrugged as if in resignation. "I'm weak. New things are so pretty, you know? And so easy. I suppose I should know better."

"I like it," I said. "I used to hate Volvos, but now I think they're all right. They don't mean what they used to mean."

"Let's get something to eat," Rachel said. She was sitting in the front seat. I was in back. She tapped on the window as we passed a Sonic. "Let's get one of those."

"You don't want one," Kelsey said. "They make 'em out of hair."

"And beaks," I said. "Lots of beaks. Ground up."

"Ground beaks, Dad," Rachel said. "I get it. That's real funny, Dad." She turned and hung her arms over the seat back. "We ought to get something, though, don't you think? Aren't you hungry?"

"I don't know," I said.

"You don't know if you're hungry or not? Don't be dumb, O.K.?" She slapped my knee. "Well, are you or aren't you?"

"It might not be such a great night for the zoo," Kelsey said. "There's too much moon, probably."

"Yeah. We were just going there as an excuse," Rachel said. "Let's eat instead. I'd rather eat. I want a chicken burger or a chicken pizza."

"No such thing," I said.

"Doesn't matter," she said. "I still want it."

The next evening Cindy Brown brought a bag of food and a two-liter bottle of Tab to the Ramada. I'd just finished watching *Nightly News* and I was standing in front of the television, my hand on the knob, ready to turn off the sound, when I noticed her peeking through the half-drawn curtains. I let her in, then dragged the curtains out to the edges of the window. It was still light.

"I wanted to see how you were getting along," she said.

"Fine," I told her.

She pushed the bag she was carrying out in front of her, held it out like a priest ready to elevate a chalice, then went into the bathroom and brought out a hotel towel, which she spread on the dark little table by the glass. She hoisted the Tab bottle out of the bag, then unwrapped a dished paper plate heaped with fried chicken. She put the plate on the table. "Jump in," she said, picking up a drumstick. She nibbled while I stared at the chicken, choosing a piece. "So, what are you waiting on?" She wiggled the leg at me as if it were a wand. "I haven't seen Theo."

I moved the Tab bottle to the far side of the table. "This looks really good, Cindy."

"Clare called to borrow my hair curler, so I figure they're doing O.K."

"Great news," I said. I pulled a wing off a small breast and started to eat, sitting on the edge of the bed.

She chewed her chicken and watched me turn the wing around, trying to figure out where to start. "I can't tell you what to do. I wish I could." She shrugged. "I can't even tell me what to do, most of the time."

I nodded, biting into the chicken.

"You like it?" She waved the leg again. "Duncan thinks my chicken's too hot, so I don't make it for him anymore."

"How's old Duncan doing?"

"Oh, he's fine. He's always fine. Get him a hat and he's a happy man. Like me and pills."

I went to the bathroom and got some glasses for the Tab. "Do you want ice? Or can you do without?"

She dropped the drumstick bone into the brown sack, which she'd put on the floor alongside her chair, then took one of the glasses and held it out. "Just give me a couple inches," she said. Then she smiled and lowered her head, pressing her forehead on her arm. "What I mean is..."

I poured the Tab too fast and then had to watch the foam edge up to and over the lip of the glass. "Oops," I said.

"Got it," she said, leaning forward to lick the mouth of the glass and then, after she switched hands, her fingers.

She was wearing a light-tan blouse, thin and very loose. Her breasts rocked under the fabric as she shook her fingers dry. "Nice shirt," I said, when I saw she'd caught me staring.

She looked down at the front of the blouse. "I've had it a long time, but don't ever wear it. It's a little, you know..."

"It is, isn't it?" I poured my Tab, then sat down again.

"Maybe I ought to behave myself here, be more neighborly."

"Do you have to?" she said.

I stopped drinking and glanced at her over the rim of my glass. She didn't change her expression. I pulled the glass away from my mouth and swallowed. "Probably," I said.

"I guess you're right." She took another piece of chicken off the pile and eased back into her chair. "Duncan says you shouldn't have left so quickly. He says you should have stayed and fought for what belonged to you. Meaning the house, I think."

"You hope," I said. I reached for a thigh that was about to fall off the plate. "There wasn't anything to fight about. It's not that kind of problem. It's no good telling her she wants me there when she wants me out."

Cindy gave me a serious look from behind her chicken, then bent forward and used the corner of the towel that was draped over the table to wipe her mouth. "Forgot something. Sorry."

"Anyway, if I had convinced her, we wouldn't have this big chance of ours." I swept my hand toward the motel room.

"Umm," she said, holding the chicken close to her face so she could inspect it. "I'd almost forgotten it." She opened her arms, resting her elbows on the arms of the chair, the chicken dangling between her right thumb and forefinger. "But, uh, you don't want to, uh, take advantage of this opportunity or anything, do you?"

I looked at her and then at the chicken I was about to eat. I dropped the thigh on the plate, then reached for it when it rolled off the top of the pile onto the towel. "What I want isn't what I'm going to do," I said.

"That's what I thought," she said. "Something to think about." She gave me a strained good-natured look, and then, without moving anything but her fingers, flipped her second chicken bone into the bag.

* * *

Joel called later and said Nassar had a place I could have
on a monthly deal, starting on the first, which was two days
away, and did I want it? I told him I did. "Great," he said.
"I figured you would. I've got to call him back now. You
hang in there, O.K.?"

I said I was fine.

The next morning I made friends with the fat guy who'd
bought the beach ball for his girlfriend. He worked for Philip
Morris and he was supposed to be on his way to Miami for
a big meeting, but something had gotten fouled up and he
had to lay over for a couple of days. His name was Pete
Peterson and he was from Salt Lake City. When we sat by
the deserted pool he wore black gym shorts and a white
short-sleeve shirt, one of those Mexican shirts that barbers
used to wear, with the square bottom, jacket-style pockets,
and narrow white pleats running down the front. His had
flowers mixed in with the pleats.

He asked about me and I told him, but I made it out to
be funny, as if Theo and I always had fights that ended up
at the Ramada Inn. He grinned as if he understood perfectly.

"Gonna be all right, Hank," he said. "I feel it in my
bones." He paused for a minute, looking at his legs. "And
that takes some doing. What you ought to do is call her
up—what's her name? Theo? What's that, short for something?"

"Theodore," I said.

"Wanted a boy, hey? You'd be surprised how many
people I meet got wrong names. Met this boy in Mississippi
once was called Basil. He worked on air conditioners. I
mean—Basil. But Theo's not bad. I don't think I'd of kissed
ass for it as a kid, though, if I was her." He squinted at me.
"Theo," he said. "It's kind of pretty. Isn't that what they
used to call Kojak?"

I nodded and said I liked it anyway.

"It doesn't matter," he said. "Look at that one, will you?"
He sat up in his plastic-web chair and craned his neck for
a look at a girl in a short red skirt who had come out of the

office to talk to a young guy who was washing the restaurant windows. "I'd like to thunder through her pass, I'm telling you." He leaned back and propped his feet against the pool ladder. "Now what we've got to do for you," he said, "is figure out what's eating Theo."

"The current program is to wait her out," I said.

"Naw, naw. Hell, you can't wait her out, she's a woman. You got no chance there. I mean, you got about as much chance as a fat boy like me with this tiny thing in red over here." He waved his drink at the girl by the restaurant. "No. You've got to develop a plan of action. Attack the problem directly. See if you can't give her what she wants. You tried flowers? Flowers kill 'em every time. Most times, anyway. Unless we got some worldwide dilemma going on. Just let me think a minute here."

While he was thinking I said, "I don't think it's going to last forever. She's a strange woman."

"No shit. I talked to this guy once, up in Chicago, had a real happy marriage, been going on for a long time and everything. I was having some trouble with the wife just then, so I asked him how he did it. You know what he told me? Said every time the baby took a dump he was right on top of it with a trowel. Said his wife never saw a thing." Peterson slapped his thigh, then brushed something off the tail of his Mexican shirt. "I don't know that that's such a great idea, but it worked for him. I didn't have a kid, so it wasn't much use to me. You got a kid?"

"Theo has. Daughter. Thirteen. She's been up here. You may have seen her."

"I been seeing a lot. The kid. That dish with the Volvo. And now last night this other workhorse."

"My neighbor. She brought fried chicken. There's plenty left if you want some."

"Is it any good? I could eat something good right about now." He looked over at the girl in red, then back at me. Then he grinned. "You got it wrapped up and everything?"

"Sure. I'll bring it down."

I went to the room and got Cindy's bag of chicken and a couple of the smaller towels that were hanging over the shower rod. When I got back downstairs the fat guy was over by the restaurant, talking to the girl. He brought her with him when he saw me. "Let's get this pretty young thing into a chair, hey?" He pointed toward a folded chair that was on its back in a two-foot brick planter on the other side of the pool.

I got the chair.

"Winnie," he said, as I came back. "Meet Henry. Henry, this is Winnie. She works here in the restaurant. I've been keeping my eye on her for a couple of days." He turned to the girl, put his big arm around her, and said, in a stage whisper, "Henry's having some problems at home. I think he needs your advice."

"Nobody needs my advice. Except maybe this brain drain we've got cleaning the glass." She jerked her head toward the window washer. "He's over there using saltwater, I mean water with salt in it—can you believe that?"

"We believe anything, don't we, Hank?"

"We do," I said.

Winnie took the chair I'd been sitting in, and I opened the new one and put it beside hers. "What's in the bag?" she said.

I still had the bag in my hand. "Food." I tossed it in a nice loop to Pete Peterson, who caught it with an exaggerated effort.

"Dan Pastorini," he said, pointing at me. "What a gun." He turned to the girl. "One of his neighbors brought him a sack of fried chicken. That's how much trouble he's got."

"Something wrong with the house chicken?" Winnie glanced at me, then turned back to Peterson, as if to make sure he knew the question was for him. She watched him unroll the top of the sack. "O.K., don't answer." She turned back to me. "Are you having problems? Or is this part of Lobo's routine?"

"Well, sure. Isn't everybody?"

"I'm sorry. It's no fun." She patted my arm. "Your friend apparently thinks I'm a party girl. That's how come he trundled me over here."

"Matchmaker," Peterson said, talking with a mouthful of fried chicken. "I'm looking out for everybody's best interest. Want some?" He held the bag out to Winnie, and, when she shook her head, rattled the bag at me. "Hank?"

"I had some already," I said.

"He already had some," Peterson said, talking into the open top of the sack. "Left me gizzard and bone."

"Oh, he did not," Winnie said, snatching the bag out of Peterson's hands. "Let me look." She stuck her hand into the bag.

He pulled the bag away from her. "Don't fiddle with the merchandise. You take care of the home boy there. I'll eat for both of us."

She shook her head. She was a young girl, maybe nineteen, with long auburn hair and skin that was slightly scarred. She said, "Let's ignore him. My name is Winnie, like the Pooh, in fact my father told me I was named after him— Pooh, I mean. I work in the restaurant here, I guess I'm sort of the assistant manager. I was married once already, but that didn't work after a year. He sold balloons, was a balloon salesman. You'd be surprised what they get for balloons nowadays. You want to go in?" She gestured to the pool.

"I don't think so," I said, smiling at her.

"I never do, either. I hate this water. They put junk in to kill everybody's germs. It'll eat the skin right off your face. I wouldn't go in there if you paid me."

Peterson finished his second piece of chicken and piled the bones on the edge of the yellow metal table alongside his chair. "You got bugs too," he said. "At night. They come around here to get burned to death. I've been watching."

Winnie rolled her eyes and said, "Oh, Pete."

"That's my name," he said. "Don't wear it out." Then

he laughed and dug into the bag for another piece of chicken. "This is great." He pointed at me with the new piece. "I think you ought to marry this woman."

"Which woman?" Winnie said.

"Why—you, of course." He peeled the skin off the chicken, looked at it for a second, then put it in his mouth.

Winnie got up, brushed her skirt, and straightened her blouse. "Thank you, Mr. Peterson. Now I've got to go in." She reached for my hand. Her palm was wet. "I'm going to get a hose for your friend here, clean him up."

O N MY last night at the Ramada, Rachel and Kelsey took me out to eat at Burger King. I got a window table while they waited in line to order the food. The table was small and yellow, the seats plastic shells mounted on square metal tubing. I sat with my feet in the aisle. There were three families in the restaurant, young couples with two children each. They ate busily. I watched the kids and listened to the teenager at the counter repeat short orders into the microphone that curled out of the cash register. She was talking to people working right behind her, six feet away, but because of the sizzling machinery, and the ice dropping into cups, and the hiss of tissue paper folding around hamburgers, they couldn't hear her without the mike.

The guy in the booth closest to my table stuck his hand out at me, pointing to something on my table. He had a mouthful of hamburger, so he couldn't tell me what he wanted. I tried the napkins first, pointing to the dispenser in the center of the table. He shook his head. I tried the salt, then the pepper, and finally hit on the ketchup. That was it. I grabbed the squirt bottle and held it out toward him.

"Thanks," he mumbled, accidentally spitting out a bit of lettuce. Instantly, he reached for his mouth, and the ketchup bottle, which I had just released, fell, bottom first, and hit the floor, shooting a short red arc out its pointed end. His kids started laughing, and then the other kids in the place, seeing what was going on, started laughing, too. Pretty soon everybody was laughing, even the guy who had asked for the ketchup. He had covered his mouth with a napkin and he was wiping and laughing at the same time. The manager, a black guy with dreadlocks and an oversize yellow name tag that said MEAT PATROL in big purple letters and MANAGER in smaller letters below, came out of the kitchen to see what was so funny.

"I was passing the ketchup," I said, pointing to the guy with the napkin.

"Uh-huh," the manager said.

I started to explain about the thing the guy had spit out, but then I thought better of it. Kelsey and Rachel had come over, too. They were right behind the manager. Rachel whispered something to Kelsey and then gestured to me, pointing toward the door. I shook my head at her.

"Sorry," I said to the black guy. "An accident."

He looked at me and then at the guy in the booth, and then he looked at the ketchup on the floor. "Uh-huh," he said. He turned and waved at a pretty girl who was peeking out of the kitchen, holding the door open five or six inches.

She came out, wiping her hands on her brown-and-gold dress. "Yes sir?" she said.

"Put some napkins on that, will you?" he said. "Then see if you can find Robo and tell him we got one. O.K.?"

"Yes sir," she said.

By this time Rachel and Kelsey were at the door. Kelsey had two Burger King bags in her hands. Rachel was pushing a french fry into her mouth, and she had a couple more in her hand. I motioned for them to come over to the table. Rachel motioned for me to come over there. I snapped my fingers at her, and the manager, who was just then going back into the kitchen, spun around and said, "You talking to me?"

I wagged a finger and then pointed toward Rachel and Kelsey. "Them," I said.

He looked and nodded, the hair bouncing around his head. Then he went back into the kitchen, leaving the pretty girl squatting over the mess, carefully placing tiny napkins in a row on top of the ketchup.

Kelsey led Rachel to the table. "Pretty exciting out here," she said. "You get mad or something?"

"Passed the ketchup," I said.

"Always a dangerous thing to do," she said.

"You did a great job, Dad," Rachel said. She got more french fries and crammed them into her mouth. "So how do you like being single? You get to go around with us a lot if you're single."

"I'm looking forward to it," I said, peering into one of the bags. "Which one's mine?"

Kelsey elbowed me out of the way and then gave me a box with a hamburger in it. "Meat and bun. How can you just eat meat and bun?"

"Yeah," Rachel said. "I like 'em wet and wild." She peeled back the top of her hamburger and showed us what was inside.

"Rachel," Kelsey said. "Put it away, please. If your father doesn't want junk on his hamburger he sure doesn't want to look at the junk on yours."

Rachel twisted the hamburger around so she could stare at its insides. She picked out a ring of onion and lowered it playfully into her mouth, then smiled at me, showing the onion.

I grinned, showing her a mouthful of hamburger.

"Oh, sick," Rachel said, covering her mouth and pretending to vomit on the table.

I caught the guy in the booth rolling his eyes toward the ceiling. When he noticed that I was looking, he rubbed his face, acting as if there was something in his eye. I watched him. He carried on the act for a long time, first with one hand, then with the other. Then he tapped his wife's shoulder and asked her to take a look. When she didn't find anything—I couldn't hear them talking, but it was clear what was going on—he got angry and pushed her, I guess trying to get her out of the way so he could go look at his eye in the men's room. She tripped on the square tubing under the booth and landed on her seat on the floor, looking surprised. She missed the ketchup, but the young girl with the napkins was so startled that she fell over backwards, smacking her head against the edge of one of the plastic seats.

The guy was suddenly solicitous, helping up his wife, brushing off her slacks. He said he was sorry, he kind of whispered it, turning away from our table, talking into her neck, but, because the restaurant had gotten quiet when the woman hit the floor, everyone in the place heard his apology.

The waitress tried to get up, awkwardly latching onto the back of the chair and hoisting herself with one hand while holding her head with the other. She didn't make it.

Now the wife was mad. She bumped the guy off her and stepped over the line of napkins to see about the waitress.

"I think it's bleeding," the girl said, pulling her hand off her head to check for blood. There wasn't any blood. "It feels like it's bleeding."

The guy's wife got behind the girl and started pawing through her hair, pushing clumps of it aside to get at the scalp. "We're O.K. here," she said. "I don't see anything."

"I'm really sorry," the husband said. He knelt in front of the girl, wiping at one of her sneakers where it had skidded on the ketchup. She wiggled her foot, yanking the shoe away.

"Leave her alone, will you?" his wife said. "What are you doing down there, anyway?"

Then the manager came busting out of the kitchen. "Who are you people?" he said, almost shouting. "What are you doing?" He picked up the waitress by the shoulders and pointed her toward the kitchen, giving her a little push. "Anna," he said to another uniformed girl who had come out of the kitchen with him. "Take her out back and walk her. See if she's O.K."

Anna waved and then grabbed the girl's arm, steering her into the kitchen.

"So," the manager said, turning back to the guy and his wife. "What is this, your living room?"

"I slipped," the wife said. "You've got damn ketchup all over the damn floor, and I slipped on it. It's not my fault."

"I'm working on the ketchup," the manager said. "And you didn't slip anyway. I saw the whole thing from over there by the terminal. Don't tell me you slipped."

"Hold on," the husband said. He was smiling, ready to make up. "Let's take it easy here. Nobody's hurt. You're not hurt, are you, Honey?" He rubbed his wife's shoulder. "Naw. You're fine." He turned and pointed to his kids, then to the door. "Let's head out," he said to them.

The kids reluctantly slid out of the booth, still sucking their milk shakes.

"Take the drinks," the guy said. "Stay in the car."

The two kids, both boys, marched out, grinning and punching each other in the arm, heads bent over their straws.

"Well, I could've slipped on the ketchup," the woman said. "I could've ruined these trousers." She twisted around to inspect the back of her pants.

"You could've broken a hip," her husband said.

The black guy gave them a stone face. "Anna?" he called, still looking at the couple. "Teresa?"

"Yes, sir?" It was Anna again. She came back into the dining area carrying an orange towel. The towel was wet, dripping.

"Get me two booklets," the manager said. "Five dollar."

"Yes, sir," Anna said. She plopped the towel on a table top and went around to the front counter.

"I want you to have these gift certificates," the manager said to the guy.

The three of them stood there for a minute without saying anything, looking at each other, until Anna came back with the booklets. She handed them to the manager, who handed them to the wife. "It's really not necessary," she said. "But it's very kind." She gave a booklet to her husband.

"I think we should be kind to each other," the manager said.

"Me too," the husband said. He pocketed the gift-certificate book.

"Too little is known about kindness," the manager said.

The husband hooked his wife's arm and the two of them started for the door. The manager watched them go. They were just about outside when the husband stopped and grabbed his shirt pocket. "You know," he said, talking across the room to the manager. "Is there any reason we shouldn't go ahead and use these now?" He turned to his wife, pulling out the gift book. "Get a little something to go? Fried pie?"

On the drive back to the Ramada Kelsey was quiet and I was quiet. Rachel asked a couple of questions, but didn't wait for answers. They dropped me in the parking lot near the stair closest to my room and I watched them drive off. It was eleven o'clock. The curtains were shut in most of the motel windows. I was halfway upstairs before I remembered there wasn't anything to drink in my room, so I came down again, searching my pants pocket for change. I had a quarter and four nickels. Not enough. I stopped by the soft-drink machine deciding whether to go to the lobby for change or forget it and go to bed. A chilly wind cut through the breezeway. There was a slight industrial smell to it, greasy and pungent, just enough to taste. The concrete where I was standing was damp, stained. I heard the engines of big trucks on the highway nearby as the drivers went up through the gears. I stayed at the machine for several minutes, jingling my change and thinking about Theo, thinking of fall nights going back ten years—Theo and me in the car going to the grocery or the drugstore, on an evening just after the summer, one of those first nights of fall when the heat evaporates suddenly and you click off the air conditioner, roll down the car windows, and let the air flood in. The air has a peculiar dense fragrance then, it wraps itself around you, chills you even though it isn't cold, freshens things instantly, and the dashboard lights are magic and eerie, glowing through the white speedometer numerals, and the tires on a parked Cadillac you notice are wholesome and pretty, and the stoplight, strung above the intersection on thick, glinting cables, seems to swagger just for you.

I GOT the key to my apartment about noon on Friday, drove back by the Ramada and checked out, then made a trip to the house to pick up some clothes. Theo had put together a box of things—kitchen stuff, towels, sheets—for me to take. The house was spotless, cleaner than it had been since we bought it. What had been Clare's room was now set up as an office, with a desk, bookshelves, and a couple of typewriters. I took a look around and went out the back door. The hole was gone.

Armstrong, who had been in his yard trimming bushes when I arrived, waved at me when I got out to the car. I waved back and dumped the clothes and the cardboard box into the back seat.

"Hold on there," he shouted, loping across the street. I put the car in reverse, but stopped toward the end of the drive. "You going for a trial separation or what?" He squatted beside the door, holding on to the mirror.

I shrugged, put the lever in park, and let the car settle in the driveway. "Looks like it."

"Bad idea. That your idea, or hers?"

He was sweaty. When he took his hand off the door mirror I watched the bubbles he left behind. I said, "More of the same. Both, I guess. I've got an apartment. I'm going to stay there awhile. How's Mrs. Armstrong?"

"She's not well. She's elderly, as you know. I expect trouble when they get that old—she's eighty-four come April." He tapped the side of the car. "But how about you? I knew it was wrong letting the old one move in. They flip-flop on you? I'll bet that'd make me feel poorly. Oh, I know. They do it from time to time."

110

I shook my head and looked out the passenger-side window at an oak that shaded most of our front lawn. "I don't think that's it, Mr. Armstrong. We're taking a little time off, is all. I've got a place over at the Nile Apartments, and I'll stay there until we get things sorted out."

"Oh, I didn't mean anything," he said, wiping his brow with the inside of his wrist. He studied the wrist for a minute. "Sure you are. Well—I've been keeping an eye on things for you. Things've been pretty quiet so far. Just the three of them, mostly."

"Yep," I said.

He looked into the back seat. "Taking some clothes, huh? That's a good-looking shirt." He rapped on the back window. "That black one there. That a Western shirt?"

I turned around to see which shirt was on top of the pile. "I'd forgotten about that. That's about an eight-year-old shirt."

"I like them pearly buttons. Those real pearl or what?" He reached in the window and fingered the shirt cuff. "Snaps," he said. Then he pulled his arm out and stepped back from the car, patting the top of the door with his palm. "I wanted to say howdy, that's all. Tell you we're all rootin' for you."

"Thanks," I said. I pulled the gear lever down into reverse and the car lurched back. I pressed the brake pedal, then swung the car out into the street.

Armstrong stood in the drive, wiping his face with his wrist. "O.K.," he said.

The apartment was a furnished two-bedroom overlooking a big square courtyard full of colored plaster animals, old signs, and fist-size white rocks. Dewey Nassar, the guy who owned the Nile, spent a lot of time rearranging the things he had—trying an ESSO sign against some white ceramic birds with long yellow legs, putting an aluminum pyramid in the center of a circular flowerbed that was dotted with large plastic pineapples. There were forty-six apartments in the four buildings he'd built in 1953 after his mother had taken him on a trip to Cairo. She'd always wanted to go, he told me once. When he returned he made a deal with some family friends, bought the land, and started planning. It was all his work, right down to the camels in the peach-colored stucco and the carnival-striped awnings. Along with the birds and the pineapples, the courtyard featured a kidney-shaped pool, three doghouses—one each in red, blue, and yellow—and palms, skinny, wretched-looking things with hairy bits of growth at their tops. There were two fountains—a small one shaped like a crescent moon, and a second one in which the water shot out of a greenish fish that was supposed to look as if it was flying.

The most recent addition to his collection of artifacts was a life-size papier-mâché steer that he'd put by the pool, head jutting over the water so it looked as if the steer had just quit drinking. Nassar hand-lettered "OFFICE" on the animal's side, and painted a fancy arrow pointing toward his apartment. From ten in the morning until ten at night Nassar played music—Middle Eastern style, with the odd big-band tune thrown in to get the natives off balance—through brown speaker horns that hung from the building eaves. And at night, every night, floodlamps splashed gaudy light across the courtyard and on the sides of the buildings. The complex had become, over the years, a minor architectural landmark, and he never had much trouble getting or keeping tenants.

Rachel and Kelsey were waiting for me on the metal stairs leading to my new apartment. "Neat place, Dad," Rachel said, waving as I crossed the courtyard.

"Glad you like it. Aren't you supposed to be in school?"

"I took the day off so we could help you move."

Kelsey was a couple of steps below Rachel. She was wearing a chrome-yellow halter and cut-off jeans with the pockets hanging out the leg openings. There was a square two-layer cake with bright white icing on the step alongside her.

I pointed to the cake. "What's that?"

"Present," Kelsey said.

"We made it together," Rachel said. "Well, really Kelsey made it, but I worked on the icing some."

"The icing's perfect," Kelsey said. "And one hundred percent yours." She looked sexier than usual, or maybe I just looked harder. "A cake always makes me feel better," she said. "Like when I'm in a new place or something. It kind of connects me with things."

"That's real nice, thanks. You want to go up and see what this dump is like?"

"We already looked in the window," Rachel said. "I saw a mouse." She swung to her feet using the railing to pivot, then went up the stairs.

"You didn't see a mouse," Kelsey said. She looked at me. "She didn't see a mouse, really."

I grinned at her. "Makes no difference to me at all. I'm not mouse-sensitive ever since I spent a week at Theo's brother's. I stayed up all night out there, slept in the kitchen so I could watch the mice run around on the dishes. This one mouse went into the big orange frying pan that we'd used to fry chicken and he got stuck in the grease."

"He likes mice. I forgot," Rachel said.

"So what happened?" Kelsey said.

I put a hand on her shoulder and stopped her at the top of the steps. "Breakfast. Mice and eggs."

"That's funny, Dad," Rachel said. "But it won't be when this guy in here gets lost in your orange juice." She banged on the door. "Open up, O.K.?"

In the kitchen Kelsey found three square plastic plates and some glasses. She brought them in and served cake and water in the living room. The furniture was a couch and two armchairs, all three pieces covered in brown and orange—a big plaid. There was a brown plastic Parsons table and there were a couple of barstools with swivel seats and, next to the kitchen, an alcove with a glass-topped dining table that had painted metal legs the diameter of coffee cans. The apartment was similar to the one Clare and I had lived in years before.

"I like it," Rachel said. "It looks like the motel."

It looked peculiar to me, maybe a little lonelier than I had hoped. I ate my cake and stared at Kelsey's legs, which were a lovely cinnamon brown and stretched out across the corner of the parson's table. I caught her eye after a minute and she sat up and crossed her legs, the left one over the right. That didn't help. If anything it made things worse, because then I stared at the taut muscle at the back of her knee and at the skin, which had a sheen to it. I got up and went into the kitchen for more water.

"So what about Mom and Clare?" Rachel worked on her empty plate, scraping at it with the fork.

Kelsey shut her eyes. "These young people today," she said, sighing.

"It's O.K. for you to be clever," I said. "But let's don't be tasteless. Theo and Clare are friends right at the moment."

"I know that," Rachel said. "What do you mean?"

Kelsey got up and took her plate, and Rachel's, into the kitchen. "He means we're all nervous but we're going to make the best of the situation by keeping our mouths shut and hoping. Isn't that what you mean?"

"More or less," I said.

"Great," Rachel said. She picked at something on her knee. "It's no big deal to me," she said.

I spent the weekend alone in the apartment. There wasn't much to do—I got my clothes into the closet and then went to Wilson's and bought a small color television, a Panasonic, which I watched all day Saturday and most of Sunday. When I wasn't watching television I was in bed, fully dressed, thinking. When that seemed self-indulgent I got up and watched more television.

Nassar knocked on the glass sliding door at about six Sunday evening. He was waving a big plastic bag that had a tropical fish in it, a blue fish. "Looky here," he said, when I opened the door. "Brought you a surprise." He thrust the bag at me.

"What is it?" I said.

"It's a blue gourami. You don't know a blue gourami when you see one? How is it possible for a person in the twentieth century not to recognize a blue gourami anymore?"

Nassar was bigger than I remembered, and more seedy-looking. The thick clump of black hair that used to be on top of his head was gone, but he still had a swatch above each ear. "You got me," I said.

We shook hands and I reached for the fish, but he drew back. "Maybe I'd better hang on until we get him settled. You got a bottle around here?" I followed him into the small kitchen. He put the bag on the counter, and the bag flattened into an oystery shape, forcing the fish onto its side. Nassar started going through the box of kitchen stuff Theo had prepared for me. "I sure am glad you're here," he said. "What's this?" He held up a mixing bowl wrapped in newspaper.

"Looks like a bowl," I said.

He unwrapped it. "I remember this. This is Clare's, isn't it?"

"I don't think so. She may have one like it. It's not a rare bowl, I don't think."

Nassar liked Clare. When we lived at the Nile she used to clip stories about Egypt out of the newspaper and out of magazines, and once a week she'd trot over to his place and deliver. He loved that. He was nuts about Egypt. When Clare left me for the would-be jeweler, Nassar was almost as upset as I was. He let me know that I was stupid to let her get away like that, and that his life, too, had been impoverished by her departure. "I recognize it," he said, holding the bowl up to get it closer to the light. "It's hers."

"Let's forget the bowl, O.K.?"

"Anything you say." He put it on the counter alongside the blue gourami. The fish jerked to the opposite side of the bag. Nassar flattened his hand and swam it around inside the bowl. "Plenty of room here. You know, I figured Clare was back to stay when she picked up with Joey." He squeezed my shoulder. "But then you come around and things mess up."

"Thanks," I said.

"Just kidding," he said. "Hey, listen—what do you say we get this guy fixed up and then head out for a little drive?"

"Sounds good." That was the truth. I was ready to go anywhere just to get out of the apartment, and a drive with Dewey Nassar, while not my idea of heaven, was still better than more television. "Where's Mariana? Maybe she wants to go?"

"I haven't seen her." He rinsed the bowl under the tap and then filled it with fresh water. "I don't think he's going to like this, you know, where he can't see out."

"He's got to like it better than the bag."

Nassar poured the water out of the bowl. "Nope. Won't work. He'll hate it. Haven't you got any kind of bottle?" He opened the refrigerator. "What about this orange juice thing? Not much in it." He got the quart bottle out and shook it to remix the juice. "I'll drink it off. That be O.K. with you?"

He drank the juice and then we emptied the bag, fish and all, into the bottle. He said, "Looks good. He's cramped in there, but it's better than the other."

The fish was floating at an odd angle to the horizontal, tail up. "He doesn't look happy," I said.

"Naw, he's fine. He's great. He's just looking around, getting things settled." He took the bottle into the living room and put it on the parson's table.

"I think he's dying," I said.

Nassar moved over to the door and looked out at his

courtyard. "So what do you think? Quite a change, huh? Lots of new stuff."

"It's amazing," I said.

"I wanted to get a real cow," he said. "A tame one. You know how you can cut a cow's hair into letters? That's what I wanted. Wouldn't that be something?"

We went for the drive in Nassar's car, a metallic blue Hudson from the late forties. He was an erratic driver, sometimes going so slow that the people behind us honked and then yelled as they scooted past, sometimes squealing the tires around ordinary subdivision corners. After thirty minutes or so he asked me if I wanted to drive. "You go ahead and take her for a while." He pulled over and rammed the curb on my side of the street with the Hudson's right front tire.

I took us back past the university. At the light a huge hook-and-ladder truck swung past us. Nassar pushed himself forward on the seat. "Let's go," he said.

"You want to follow the truck?"

"He may be headed out toward Blue Gardens, my new apartments. Come on, turn this baby around." He slapped the dash a couple of times for emphasis.

I drove through a Gulf station and bounced us back out into the street heading the opposite direction, nearly killing a fat girl who was riding some kind of motor scooter. We were right behind her and there wasn't any way to go around—all the cars in the left lane had stopped for somebody ahead who was trying to make a turn across the traffic.

"Hit the horn," he said. "Blow her damn ears off. What's she think she's doing, anyway? He reached in front of me and punched on the horn rim. "What a pig," he said.

The girl didn't budge. She was wearing a huge candy-apple red helmet and rubbery-looking toreador pants, and her rump hid the seat. I tapped the horn a couple of times.

"What're you, Mr. Refinement? Hit the damn thing," Nassar said, reaching to press the rim again. He leaned on it this time, and the girl, who was only ten feet or so in front of us, calmly reached behind her back and shot us the finger.

"Thanks, Sweetie," Nassar said, and slid back into his seat.

"Here's the problem up here," I said, lifting my chin at the windshield. "Guy turning left. We'll get her there."

"Forget it. We've lost the truck now anyway. Besides, I'm insured up the ass."

When we got alongside the girl Nassar waved at her and she flipped up the visor that covered the front of her helmet. She was fat all right. And she wore sunglasses under the visor, so even when it was out of the way we couldn't see her eyes.

"Why don't you pick on something your own size?" Nassar yelled out the window. The girl's face didn't change. I couldn't tell whether or not she'd heard him. He yelled it again, louder this time.

She looked back and forth between us and the road. Still there wasn't any expression on her face. She was just watching us. Nassar turned around to me and said, "Can you believe this woman? We ought to give her a little nudge. Maybe that'd get a rise out of her. I shouldn't do this, should I?"

"She's doing all right," I said. I sped up some, thinking that would take care of things. But when I sped up, she did, too.

Nassar stuck his head out the window. "Sorry," he shouted. He brought his hands up alongside his face and opened them toward heaven as if he were a church statue. "It got away from me for a minute." Then he came back inside the car. "Hang a left anytime," he said.

The next cross street was blocked with orange saw horses that were there to prevent people from driving off a two-foot cliff into the red clay of a new roadbed. The street after had a light that was just turning amber. I started to try and make the light, but it was red and the intersection was full of cars by the time I was halfway through the block. I slowed quickly, trying to make the girl pass me, but she didn't bite. When we stopped she put both feet down and took her hands off the handlebars. Nassar hung out the window again and pointed ahead of us. "We were chasing this fire truck," he said, and then he shrugged.

The girl unzipped her jacket, which was green and made of leather-look vinyl. Her face was kind of bulging inside the helmet. She pulled a pistol out of the jacket and fired at our front tire. Then she said, "Hiya, Bozo."

I hit the accelerator and spun the steering wheel to the left, then jammed on the brakes so I wouldn't smash into a Honda coming the other way. Nassar got down on the seat. The girl flipped her visor shut and walked the scooter forward, edging up on the light.

The air was out of the tire instantly, pitching the Hudson forward and to the right. Nassar peeked over the dashboard. "Gracious. She's pissed, isn't she? I tried to apologize, didn't I? Jesus."

"I think I'll just poke along here over to the left," I said, letting out the clutch and swinging the car into the driveway in front of a One Hour Martinizing place.

We got out of the car to take a look at the tire. The girl was through the intersection and almost out of sight. "She ought to be reported to the Gun Commission," Nassar said, shaking his head and staring at the tire. "I mean, Jesus— in broad daylight."

A guy in a silver Pontiac with swan decals on the driver's door pulled into the parking lot alongside us. "You all right?" he asked, looking from me to Nassar and back again at me. "I saw everything. She could've killed you."

"We're fine," I said.

"She just went crazy," Nassar said. "I don't know what happened. We were going along and then bang, she shoots us." He looked at me as if he wanted the story corroborated.

"Something like that. We were kidding her about being in the way back up here." I wagged my thumb toward the intersection where we'd seen the fire truck.

"She didn't take it too well," the guy said.

"No," I said.

The guy fished around on the seat beside him and produced a business card, which he held out the window. Nassar took the card. "This is me. If you want to press charges, call me." He grinned. "We've got to stick together."

Nassar flapped the card back and forth on the fingers of his free hand while the guy made a circle in the parking lot and drove off. Nassar looked at the card and then at me. "I don't know about this dude," he said.

I bent over the tire, inspecting the hole in the sidewall. "Have you got a spare?"

"Sure do." He went around toward the trunk. "I used to, anyway. Maybe we better check."

There was a B. F. Goodrich tire with about ten pounds of air in it in the trunk. We put that on and got back in the car, Nassar driving this time. "I've got a great idea," he said. "You want to hear a great idea?"

I wiped perspiration off my forehead with my palm. "Sure. What is it?"

"Let's get us a snack, a nice piece of pie or something. Huh? Got the spot all picked out." He swerved to miss a cat trotting along the side of the road. "You just sit back and relax. I'm going to fix you right up."

He took us back by the university and then out the highway, driving carefully. We got stuck behind a rental van and he waited patiently for a chance to pass. The highway was blacktop, recently resurfaced, with bright-yellow lane divisions, and turn arrows at each intersection. There was a gully of healthy grass separating the in and out lanes, and there wasn't much traffic. New amber streetlamps spread an eerily indirect light over the highway. I wondered where Theo was and who she was with, what she was doing.

The old car almost floated along the highway. Nassar

didn't talk. I thought of Theo's broad shoulders, of how she looked sitting in a dining chair at a restaurant, of the back of her jeans after she'd taken them in at the waist.

Nassar popped my arm. "Hey. Don't think about it. Wait'll you see what I've got."

"It creeps up," I said.

"I've got something that'll creep up. She works here." He poked a finger toward the steering wheel.

"Give me a break, will you?"

"No, listen. My wife's sister, the one with a degree in hotel management, she's at the Ramada. You probably always wondered what happened to people with degrees in hotel management."

"I hope you're kidding me."

"Who's kidding? She's a nice girl. Twenty, maybe. You know how they are at twenty."

"I must've forgotten."

He thought I wanted him to tell me, so he did. Used his hands a lot. Told me that women reach a point and then blossom. "Like larvae. Suddenly they're twenty years old, or eighteen, or twenty-six, and bam, they're beautiful. They live in another world right then. Everything seems possible."

"Yeah," I said. "You and Charles Boyer worked on that idea together."

"What's that mean?"

"Never mind. It's fine. I'd like to meet Mariana's sister. What's her name?"

He sighed theatrically. "Well, we got a problem on the name, O.K.? I'll give you that. It's Winifred. But, hey—" he bumped me again on the arm—"she's a looker."

"Winifred? At the restaurant? I met a girl named Winnie out here."

He lifted his foot off the gas and slowed the car going into the left-turn lane. "See there? You already met her. Great. We'll have a great time, huh?"

"I liked her," I said.

"Good. Now you can like her some more." He pulled

into a blue-lined handicapped parking zone in front of the lobby of the motel.

"She's a kid," I said. "That's the only problem."

Nassar swung open his door. "That ain't a problem. That's a gift from heaven—don't you know nothing?"

The lobby of the Ramada smelled bad. Nassar talked to the kid behind the counter, a teenager named Ramon who had helped me when the hot water in my room was acting up. "You know Henry?" he said to Ramon. "Henry, meet Ramon."

The kid tipped an imaginary hat at me. "You can't stay away?"

"I'm traveling with the chief here." I pointed to Nassar.

"You could do better," the kid said.

Nassar said, "You seen Winifred? She in the restaurant?"

"Beats me—oh, I get it." Ramon wiggled a finger at me and then toward the restaurant.

"The boy's fast," Nassar said.

The restaurant was empty. The chairs were burgundy vinyl studded with black-headed furniture tacks, and the carpet was red with a chocolate scroll pattern. Nassar took a booth by one of the windows that looked out on the pool.

Winnie came out of the kitchen wearing a cheesy-looking black uniform and a white apron. "Didn't you see the sign?" she said, pointing toward a table by the entrance. There wasn't any sign there. "Well, there's supposed to be a sign over here," she said, crossing toward the table she'd pointed at. "Says 'Section Closed,' or something like that."

Nassar bent toward me and whispered, "Let me handle this, O.K.?"

"What's he telling you now?" Winnie came back and stood alongside the booth we were in. "You've got the strangest friends," she said to me.

I shrugged and smiled at her.

"How about some coffee and pie?" Nassar said. "Or maybe a waffle with all the trimmings?"

"How about a polio salad," Winnie said.

Knowing she was Mariana's sister, I saw the resemblance—the hair, of course, though Winnie's was several shades lighter, and around the eyes, which were a lovely light blue. I said, "It turns out I used to live at his apartments. I've known Mariana for years."

"You lived at Nassarland?" Winnie said.

"Love the dress," Nassar said. "Makes my job a lot easier."

"We like it around here," she said, twirling to show off the uniform. "I filled in for Lorraine at the buffet. It was a dream."

"She doesn't usually wear the uniform," Nassar said to me. "She's the assistant something-or-other."

"A high post," she said. "Actually, I like the dress. It's kind of sweet and sleazy."

"Me too," I said. "The dress, I mean."

"I was wondering," Winnie said.

"He already told me he liked you," Nassar said. "So go easy."

"I'm going as easy as I can," she said. "What's wrong with how I'm going?" She did our table with a brown rag she pulled out of her apron pocket, knocking the sugar bowl and the salt shakers out of the way. "How's my sister?"

"We don't know," Nassar said. "She's probably hanging out there working on her research."

"So you came out to leer at Ardith?"

Nassar grimaced at her. "No, Pudding, I did not come out to leer at Ardith. I came out to take you and my friend Henry here to dinner. That's what."

"He's hot for this tart who works the register," Winnie said. "She's about fifty. We try to keep it from Mariana."

"Cute," Nassar said. He grabbed her rag and popped it at her a couple of times.

"Usually she's tied up with the showboats," Winnie said. "You know, wet-look hair and pointy shoes in ice-cream colors. They're polite for half a second and then they're up your skirt like a squid. Ardith likes 'em pretty much." She went across the room to pick up a ketchup packet that was on the floor near a stack of chairs. "See what I mean?" she said, sailing the packet across the restaurant toward the kitchen.

A fat guy in checked red pants peered into the restaurant. He was bald, but he had a black beard that was very carefully trimmed, ear to ear. He waved at Winnie. "Oh. Sorry," he said. "Check you later."

"The buffet's in the Coronado Room," she said. "Back past the lobby and turn left. It closed at six-thirty, but if you hurry you might find something."

"O.K. Thanks," the guy said. He waved at Nassar and me, then went out.

"He don't look healthy," Nassar said.

Winnie brought three cups of coffee to the table. "So where are we going for dinner?"

"I was thinking the Wet Club," Nassar said. "At the bay."

"Wait a minute, now," I said. "That's an hour down and an hour back, isn't it?"

"You got a tight calendar?" He slapped me on the biceps.

"Forty minutes each way," Winnie said.

"Sure. And we can take Winnie's car." He hit me again. "She's got a convertible."

Winnie got up and headed for the kitchen. "You guys figure it out," she said. "I'm seeing if Honey and Dot are in back."

Nassar watched her go, then reached across the table and grabbed my wrist. "Don't let her grill you," he said, lifting an eyebrow and tilting his head toward the kitchen. "She's young, but not that young. I thought you liked her."

"Maybe she thinks she's being set up. Maybe she doesn't want to go."

He groaned. "What, she's a loaf of bread? If she didn't want to go she'd say."

"Right," I said. I pulled out of his grip.

Winnie came through the swinging silver kitchen doors talking to a short, blocky girl in jeans and a tank top. Winnie had changed into pants and a man's shirt that was several sizes too big for her. The two of them stopped by the register for a second and laughed at something, then the girl stepped behind the checkout counter and rang the register. Winnie came across to us. "You get him squared away?"

The motel's sign was blinking and the sky behind it had turned dark gray, touched with streaks of red. We went back through town in Winnie's convertible, which was one of the new ones, a Chrysler, with the top down and the radio too loud. Nassar insisted that we all sit in front, with him driving. Winnie had to shout to be heard. "Dewey says I live wrong. Like a hippie."

"Same thing," I said.

"I've seen pictures, you know—articles about the sixties and everything. I was two then, or something."

I nodded and smelled her hair when the wind blew it into my face. The fragrance was sweet and dense, like a closed garden.

"It's just because I wear a lot of tank tops and go barefoot in summer," she said. "He's only been to my house once, and then I was moving."

Nassar was slumped low behind the steering wheel, driving with one hand and fingering his lip with the other. He caught me looking at him and winked. Winnie turned around just as he did it and she yelled something I couldn't make out into his ear. He smiled and gave her a squeeze on the thigh. Then she was back to me, talking close to my cheek. "We have to keep him interested. I told him I was hungry."

The wind was too much, finally, so I just nodded to her, smiled, and then we kept quiet, watching the road, the landscape, the other cars. We went through a small town in which all the houses had shiny bushes and soft-looking lawns bound by four-foot chain-link fences. The houses were old, from the forties, but extraordinarily well kept— lots of white paint and painted concrete porch steps. The light was coppery. The gray of the sky had gone an almost metallic red in the west. Nassar, who'd been doing seventy on the open highway, barely slowed going through the town, and then we were back out in the open. The landscape was more grassy now, lined with endless barbed-wire fences and tattered billboards advertising products that no longer showed up on TV. Every now and then there was a clump of weathered trees grouped in a half-circle around the garage of a house that looked as if it belonged in a subdivision back in town. In the distance a line of awkward metal towers paraded across the terrain like fierce and elegant Japanese warriors. Winnie gathered her hair and pulled it over her right shoulder, twisting it into a roll. "I like it," she shouted, pointing at the landscape. "It's crazy and romantic."

I nodded again, pushing aside the stray bits of her hair that were slapping at my face.

"You liked being married, didn't you?"

I smiled at her, then at Nassar, who had turned around to see what she was yelling about. "Yeah." I shrugged clumsily, wedging my upper arm against Winnie's.

She looked around at where our arms were touching, then up at me. "That's really wonderful. To feel that about being married. It almost renews a girl's faith." She pulled a green rubber band out of her shirt pocket, released and then refixed her hair, and wrapped the rubber band around the end of the twist.

We passed a brand-new shopping center, a kind of minimall and a Sears auto store spread out on several acres of black parking lot. A theater marquee in one corner of the lot read: BRING 'EM BACK ALIVE FILM FESTIVAL. Nassar reached around Winnie's back and hit my shoulder, then wagged his finger toward the sign.

When we got to the bay exit the sun was gone and all the juke joints had their signs on—the Hi Hat Club, the Green Parrot, Topper's, Redfish & Candy's, the Surf Café. Their oyster-shell parking lots were jammed with trucks and Cadillacs. The air was salty. There was the smell of fish everywhere, gas stations were selling live bait, and all the stores had fifty-gallon oil drums full of cane poles at their entrance doors.

"Almost home," Nassar hollered, and both Winnie and I nodded agreement.

We turned off the interstate onto a lesser highway, slow and crowded. People were wandering back and forth across the road, and other people were honking car horns and shouting obscenities. Vans with science-fiction paintings on their sides rolled by with guys hanging out windows and sitting in open back doors, waving cans of beer and whistling at the girls who strolled in groups through the club parking lots. The cars were creeping along the road. Somebody in a jeep called out to Winnie, asking her what she was doing with the oldsters. She gave the guy a solid fist and he laughed, then wheeled off the road and drove through the ditch into a place called the Heron, which had a covey of white neon birds flapping across its roof. There were about six radios going, filling the sudden community with rock-and-roll classics—I recognized "You're a Thousand Miles Away" and a Rolling Stones tune and "Stay," and all the people, both in and out of the cars, were moving around, bobbing and nodding to the music. Even Winnie was rocking her head back and forth.

She slapped my leg. "Hey. Get with it, Oldster."

"I'm doing O.K. It takes us a little longer to get started, is all."

She laughed. I thought how pretty she was when she laughed, how much like Rachel. "So what do you think about me so far?" she said.

Nassar was leaning forward trying to tune the radio. He heard the question and turned to me, grinning a big grin.

"I think you're terrific," I said.

A small flatbed truck with no doors pulled into the traffic in front of us. There was a sunburned girl in white overalls riding splay-legged on the plank bed, and, alongside her, a big spotted dog who was licking at a toy of some kind, something red and plastic.

Nassar nodded at me, still grinning.

We followed the truck over a steep wooden bridge with a metal grid in the center that buckled and whined when our tires rolled across. "That's nice," Winnie said. "I'm glad."

Immediately after the bridge, Nassar made a left turn onto a gravel road that went back alongside the pilings and then swerved right. The gravel was the size of golf balls and there was a lot of it. The car sank, then surged up and to one side, then straightened again, and repeated the procedure. It was clownish, the way Nassar was bulling us through, and Winnie started bouncing up and down, mimicking the car, bumping into me, then Nassar, then me again, and she was laughing about it. Every time she banged into one of us she laughed more, and pretty soon we were all laughing and bumping around, and the car waddled even more hopelessly.

There was sheet lightning off to the west, not far off, followed by a huge clap of thunder that scared us into silence. The road had gotten narrower and was boxed in on each side with beach houses built on top of telephone-pole pilings. None of the houses were lit, so it was very dark. Behind us the hump of the bridge was silhouetted by tiny bulbs strung along its arc, and by the glow from the tavern lights beyond. In front, the headlights hit a few chrome car bumpers, some bicycle reflectors nailed into poles, and the gold eyes of a cat that stopped in the center of the road, stared at us, then vanished into a gully.

Nassar stopped the car. "I think we better get the top," he said, reaching under the dash. The top made a whirring sound as it rose out of its boot behind the back seat. He lifted his foot off the brake pedal and the car inched forward.

"Dewey," Winnie said. "We're rolling."

"I planned that," he said. He latched the top and then pushed the buttons on the armrest to raise the windows.

"Cozy," Winnie said, when we were sealed inside the

car. She draped an arm over my shoulder. "I'm glad he brought you. I'm glad you like me."

I combed my hair with my fingers and then with my palm. "It is better with the windows up," I said.

"Oh, don't be silly," she said, patting me. "You're doing fine."

"You're dead, Pal," Nassar said.

Winnie rubbed my shoulder. "Don't pay any attention to my brother-in-law. We're almost there. In about half a minute I'll have you up to your thighs in lobster sauce." She pointed out the windshield at a row of what looked like Christmas decorations a couple of hundred yards ahead.

We crossed a narrow plank bridge with no rail. I said, "What's over here?" and waved to our left where it was pitch black except for a single blue bulb dangling under a corrugated-tin shed.

"Inlet," Nassar said.

Winnie leaned in front of him, staring out his window. "You can't even see it," she said. "How do you know it's there?"

"I guessed," he said. "The first time. After that I saw it in daylight." He spun the car to the left to avoid a guy in leather shorts who was on my side of the road washing his underarms at a tall spigot. "Friend of yours?"

"My father," I said.

"He's clean, anyway," Winnie said. She settled in the seat and absentmindedly messed with the radio buttons. "I like to go places with new guys," she said.

"Why don't you give him a break, Winnie," Nassar said. "Look how nice he's being, and you're pushing him around."

"Yeah, Winnie," I said. "I could be home watching TV. I could be in my living room or something, playing with my fish."

"I gave him a fish," Nassar said.

"Way to go, Dewey," she said.

The Christmas lights were Japanese lanterns strung along

a makeshift walk that ran from a fancy International-style building down to a pier. Dragonflies and gnats and mosquitoes circled the lights. Nassar bucked the car up an embankment that served as the restaurant's parking lot and we got out. There was a strong wind blowing in off the water, and there were metal things banging, and the sounds of a boat motor and of ropes straining. Nassar said, "So what do you think?"

The restaurant looked like a milk plant, or some other industrial building from the forties, that had been renovated. It was very slick. It had a fresh coat of white paint. The wall that faced the bay was curved and made out of clear glass block. The diners inside looked wavy through the glass.

"Not a bad joint, huh?" Winnie said, wrapping her arms around my waist, hugging me as we stood on the boardwalk looking at the restaurant. I hugged her back. The paper lanterns were ratcheting here and there in the wind, casting many shadows. I felt good.

We got a round table by the glass-block wall and Nassar started telling me about this piece of furniture he'd seen somewhere. "It's a highboy," he said. "You know what a highboy is? Red lacquer and paws for drawer handles, animal paws—the real thing. The top has these bells built in. The whole thing's on a hydraulic carriage, so if you even touch it the furniture floats away from you, tinkling. I was planning to put it in your apartment."

"A wonderland special," Winnie said. "Sounds like a natural." She flapped her menu at me. "What do you like?"

"Let me take a gander at this." I swept the menu off the table, opening it with a flourish that knocked over my wine glass.

Winnie caught it on one bounce off the tablecloth. "Now, Henry, let's don't get too excited," she said, putting the glass back in its spot on the table.

Nassar hit me in the arm. "Girl's got hands," he said. "Huh? We got to pump her up with a little grub here, and then speed on by the blimp ruins—you know the blimp ruins? Out by the air base? It's mondo out there at night."

"Mega-mondo," Winnie said.

Nassar's blimp ruins were the remains of a hangar—a dozen round concrete pilings and part of a wall that loomed over an old two-lane highway running parallel to the new highway. The structure looked like a ruin, the pilings like ancient totems, gray and solemn against the starry night. The three of us climbed an eight-foot fence and ignored huge U.S. GOVERNMENT trespassing signs so we could get close to where the building had been, and then, after circling the concrete apron a couple of times, we climbed the fence again and rode home in silence.

——— • ———

WINNIE STAYED at the apartment. We fell asleep watching a rerun made-for-TV movie about campus unrest in the sixties, then woke up about two and made love. It was a big success. I hadn't slept with anyone but Theo for years, so, once we got started, I went a little crazy. She liked it. I thought her stomach was amazing, her skin, her legs—everything. I had a wonderful time. At four-thirty we vowed to do it again soon, and fell asleep in each other's arms.

Monday morning it was raining hard and Winnie was gone. I made coffee and had a piece of Kelsey's cake, then sat on my ugly new couch and watched the rain. Somebody from the office called at nine to ask if I needed a ride. I said I had to wait for the gas person, which wasn't true. The gas had been turned on Friday, before I arrived.

At nine-thirty Nassar was out in the courtyard. He was wearing a yellow slicker about half his size and he was moving his ornamental birds around. I expected him to trot upstairs to see how things had gone, but he didn't. He didn't even look my way. I watched him for about ten minutes and then he disappeared back inside his apartment, which I could just see by pressing up against my sliding door.

In the kitchen, in the refrigerator, I found a note from Winnie. It said, "Great to meet you."

I called Theo. "Hi," I said. "It's Henry."

"I know," she said. "Rachel loves your apartment. She wants to live there if we fix things up. She's worried about you and Kelsey. She asked me if I thought Kelsey was sexy. I said she wasn't your type."

"Who is?" I said.

Theo made a sighing noise. "Is that a joke?"

"It was supposed to be. How's Clare? I haven't seen Joel at all."

"Clare's fine and Joel's in Constantinople or something. Kuwait, maybe."

"Oh, yeah. He told me he had another trip." I looked at my foot. "Thanks for the stuff, for packing it and everything."

"Sure. Don't you go to work anymore?"

"Not today. I'm resting. There's stuff around here to do, getting set up—you know. I figured I'd take a day off and do it." I walked to the window and saw Nassar again, this time carrying a stuffed animal out of his apartment and through the gate to the covered parking area. "You ought to come see this place sometime."

"Clare told me," she said.

I watched Nassar go back into his apartment. "So. I thought I'd call to thank you. For the stuff."

"Uh-huh." There was a clicking sound on the line. We both listened for a minute. Finally, Theo said, "Cindy's in the hospital. She tried to kill herself. She's O.K. Apparently she's done it twice. Tried, I mean. She's at Methodist, room three-forty. I'm surprised Duncan didn't call."

"Are you kidding? Jesus."

"I saw her last night and she was O.K. They were just Valium. She takes them all the time."

"She's lucky."

"Ryan O'Neal's lucky, if you want luck."

That was the end of our conversation. I got cleaned up to go to the hospital, but then my car wouldn't start. Nassar came outside just as I was lifting the hood for a look at the engine. I tested the obvious connections—the battery, the distributor—with him looking over my shoulder. "I've got a guy," he said. "Friend of mine. Runs his own shop. You want me to get him out?"

"It's an old car," I said.

"He's an old guy," Nassar said. "I'll call him." He went

back inside and left me leaning against the car's front fender.

In a few minutes a Checker cab pulled up. "You got a problem? the driver said. He was a white kid with a Mr. T haircut.

"Won't start." I raised my head toward the car.

"You want me to take a look?" He swung open his door and got out, leaving the cab running. "I can probably fix it."

"The landlord's calling somebody," I said. But the kid was already bent under the hood of my car.

"Turn it over," he said. His hand came out from under the hood and motioned toward the front seat. "Lemme hear it."

I got into the car and tried to start it. The motor turned over but wouldn't catch. I got out and went around to the front and watched him fiddle with the fuel line.

"Fuel pump," he said. "Bad one, sounds like."

"That's what I thought," I said.

He said, "Maybe somebody put a bag of sugar in the tank. Could be just about anything." He pulled himself forward and reached down alongside the engine. I couldn't see what he was reaching for, but when he got it he gave it a couple of hard twists. "Try it again," he said.

I did. The car didn't start. When I got out he was standing on the blacktop looking at the engine and wiping his hands on a flowered washcloth he must've had in his pocket. "It's O.K.," I said. "We've got a guy coming."

He shook his head. "I hope he's got a tow. This is one dead motherfuck." He started to leave. "You need a lift?"

I said I did.

The cab was clean. He had a lot of radio gear mounted under the dash, and he played with it as he drove. He got a tape out of a leather-covered box on the seat and pushed it into the cassette player. "Check this out," the kid said, and he turned the music up loud.

"Amazing," I said. I sat forward in the back seat, staring at the equalizer. "I'm headed for Methodist Hospital."

"Gotcha," the kid said, pointing at my face in the mirror with his index finger. Then he pointed at his radio. "Check the highs. It's hot for you, right? Twelve-inch poly sub-woofers in back. Rack mount. Take a look."

I looked over my shoulder at the panel at the top of the rear seat. The fabric there was quivering.

"Blowing two hundred watts through those babies. I crank up and you get a facelift."

Duncan caught my elbow coming out of the elevator on the third floor. He steered me back into the elevator. "Let's eat something. Downstairs. She's asleep." We rode down to the first floor. In the snack bar he picked out a cheese sandwich cut into two triangles and wrapped in cellophane. I borrowed a couple of quarters from him to get a Diet Pepsi out of the soft-drink machine. He ate the first half of the sandwich in three bites and decided he didn't want the rest. "I don't know," he said, rewrapping the sandwich. "This usually happens to somebody else, doesn't it?"

I smiled in a way that was supposed to look sympathetic. "I'm glad she's O.K.," I said.

"Me too. This is our third, you know." He pushed at the sandwich, moving it across the Formica tabletop as if it were a toy. "First time she used a gun and made this red scar on her shoulder right at the base of her neck." He drew a line on his neck where the scar was. "I rushed to the hospital and found her in a green chair by the bed, reading a book about trees. Her neck was bandaged and she couldn't move her head much." He shook his head. "She was disappointed because the doctor wouldn't let her stay overnight at the hospital. We went home. I took care of her, got her some-thing to eat—I even went out and got a fifty-foot coax extension for the cable and then moved the TV into the bedroom. She went to sleep and I sat up all night and watched movies without any sound. When I woke up around noon the next day she was in the kitchen frying bacon."

I snorted at that, a kind of half-laugh that was meant as an appreciation of the oddness of things. Duncan kept playing with the sandwich.

"The next time she used a bread knife. The doctor told me that saved her, the bread knife. Serrated edge. After that one we went to Santa Rosa Island for a vacation. I remember her running into the surf until she was waist deep, holding her bandages up out of the water." He held his arms up to illustrate, then rested them on the table, flicking his finger at a corner of the plastic that had detached itself from the sandwich wrapper. "I don't know what I'm supposed to do. I mean, she's fine." He looked at me, then back at the Formica. "When I was up there a minute ago she was telling me that she wanted to buy a horse. Said she'd always liked horses but they scared her, and now she figured it was time to get over that."

"So buy a horse," I said. "We could use a horse in the neighborhood."

"That's what I said. Same thing. Same line."

I nodded at him and watched him play with the plastic, then said I'd come back to see Cindy later in the afternoon, and left him in the snack bar. At the office I called Nassar to find out about my car. He told me his guy had taken it away, but that he'd promised to have it back before dark. "He doesn't have a lot to do," Nassar said.

I said that was fine.

Clare called the office in midafternoon and said she thought we ought to get together and discuss the situation. I said I was ready when she was, and she suggested a quick dinner at a place called Monroe's, which was a gas station somebody had turned into a plant-filled restaurant. She picked me up in the parking lot outside my apartment at six and we went in her car. As soon as we were inside the restaurant she excused herself and went to the ladies' room. I counted the plants. There were more than forty of them. Some were tiny things. When Clare sat down again I said, "How's Theo?"

"Good. She worries about you. I'm sorry we don't have more time. I didn't want to rush this and now I have to." She stared at the menu. "I think I'll have the squid. You probably don't want me to have it, do you? You don't care for people who eat squid. I remember."

"I've changed my position on squid," I said.

"We didn't get to talk much when you were at the house. I guess you think I did this. Theo, I mean. With the Colorado trip and everything."

"We're getting right into it?"

"Yeah. And I don't want the squid, either. This is a terrible place to eat. I came here with Joel once and there was a spider crawling on the table. I don't know why I said here."

"You want to go someplace else?"

"Nope. No time. Besides, between you and me we'd end up running around for two hours. Remember? Every restaurant we went to there was something wrong. It'd take us six places just to get a hamburger."

"I remember," I said.

"So, how are you? You want a steak? My treat."

"Just a potato. What're you doing about Joel?"

"He went to Tanzania for two weeks," Clare said. "He wants me to marry him. I told him I couldn't."

"He was going to trash me before you two went to Colorado. Ran me off the road and everything."

"He could. I saw him ruin a guy's head once."

Clare ordered the squid after all, and I got a steak to go with my potato. The food came much more quickly than it should have. "This is rubbery and tasteless," she said. "You should try it." We looked at each other for a second and then started laughing. "Well, maybe you shouldn't." She moved the squid away from the center of her plate.

"Gimme a hunk of that." She pointed at my steak with her knife.

I cut the steak in half, caught one piece between my knife and fork, and passed the steak across the table.

"Thanks," she said. She cut off a corner and put it in her mouth. "You're still O.K. Sometimes I wish I adored you the way I used to. You, or somebody, anyway. I think I preferred that."

I said, "I liked it pretty well."

She smiled. "No kidding."

"Sorry," I said, pressing my napkin into a triangle on the table top.

She finished her half of the steak very quickly, then said, "What about coffee? No, I guess not."

I waved at the waiter, who arrived at the table with the bill on a half-size cafeteria tray which he lowered and slid onto the thick white tablecloth. "Thank you, sir," the waiter said. "Will there be anything else, sir?"

I pushed my American Express card across the table with my forefinger. "No. Thank you."

"Was there some difficulty with the squid?"

Clare shook her head. "It was fine."

The waiter nodded, picked up the card and his tray, and left, moving backwards.

"That's a big tray he's got," Clare said.

We left the restaurant and when she dropped me off outside the gate at the Nile she asked what I was going to do. I told her I was going to see Cindy.

"Not what I meant," she said. "We didn't get much done, did we? At this dinner." She turned to look at me and rested the side of her head on the steering wheel. "I just wanted you to know that I didn't plan things. I'm surprised, the same as you."

I was standing in the open passenger-side door, bent at the waist so I could see her. I picked a silver gum wrapper out of the carpeted gully between the seat cushion and the door sill. I said, "I like her, too, Clare."

She pulled the gear lever down into drive, keeping her foot on the brake pedal. "I'll tell her."

The corridors on the third floor were empty when I got to the hospital. I walked on my toes so I wouldn't make any noise. A nurse stuck her head out the door of the nursing station. When she saw me, she came down the hall in a hurry, silent except for the sound of her skirt and the squeal of her shoes. She looked at her watch, then wound it. "Visiting hours are almost over," she said.

"I'm looking in on Cindy Brown," I said. "I'm her next-door neighbor."

"She's probably asleep. You shouldn't bother her."

"Just a look. That's all."

The nurse huffed, then stuck her hands in her pockets and turned quickly on her heel, indicating that I should follow her. Her turn made a small, curved scuff mark on the floor.

She left me at the door to 340, telling me to get in and get out. I thanked her and waited until she was around the corner before I went in. It was dark in the room. Cindy was on her side with her knees drawn up and her hands pushed under the pillow. She had on a blue nightgown with a ruffled collar. The light from the corridor cut through the room and folded up and over the bed, then up the wall. Cindy groaned and whispered something, then wiped one hand over her face and turned away from the light. I pushed the door closed. It was dark except for a steady stoplight-green bulb on the wall above the bed. I picked my way across the room, opened the curtains, and looked out at the thin moon. For some reason I was thinking of the feeling you get when you're handling a particularly sharp knife in the kitchen and suddenly, without really thinking about it, it's almost as if you're afraid of what your hand will do, afraid that it wants to push the point slowly into your eye. I shook the thought off and shut the curtains, then rubbed my fingers into my eye sockets, circling my eyes, which felt like overinflated footballs, hard and much larger than they should have been. I thought about that driving home.

I called Winnie. Her answering machine had a lot of classical music in the background as she patiently explained that I should leave my message at the tone, and that my message should include my name, my telephone number or numbers, the date and time of my call, and the nature of my business, if any. Then the tone came. I couldn't bring myself to say anything. I didn't want to hang up either, so I stood there with the telephone pressed against my ear for a few seconds. Finally I said, "Great meeting you too." That felt stupid. I waited for the machine to disconnect—a long time—trying to think of something else I could say to fix what I'd already said. Nothing came to me. Then I put the receiver back in its cradle and went into the bedroom, still trying to think of something. I picked up an *Audio* magazine I'd gotten at the grocery store and thumbed through the section on car stereo. I started reading a test of a Nakamichi tuner, but I couldn't concentrate. I forgot whether the signal-to-noise ratio was supposed to be high or low, so I spent a few minutes comparing the specs of different tuners, thinking that the more expensive ones would have better signal-to-noise ratios. Then I decided I didn't want a Nakamichi tuner anyway, so I put the magazine away and went into the kitchen to wash the dishes. There were three of them— a plate, a cup, and a pink bowl with small zebras on it. I'd used it for ice cream. There were several glasses. I rinsed what was in the sink and loaded the dishwasher. As I poured Cascade into the swing-out compartment in the dishwasher door I wondered if dishes got cleaner when there were so few of them—more water action, more heat, more scrubbing power to go around, I figured. I wondered if there was a dishwasher manual somewhere around. I took a look at the blue gourami. Then I called Kelsey. She answered the telephone on the fifth ring and asked if she could get back to me.

"Sure," I said, and hung up.

It was quiet outside. The courtyard looked prim and artificial, like a stage set. I went to the glass sliding doors and studied the scene. Things weren't going so well, I decided.

"**R**IGHT NOW you're what I'd call marginal," Nassar said. We were standing alongside the dumpster that he and Mariana were painting yellow. It was about noon. I'd spent the morning cleaning my apartment and I'd come out to the dumpster with a plastic bag stuffed with garbage. Nassar poked the bag with his brush. "That about a week's worth?"

"Just breakfast," I said, pulling the bag away from him.

Mariana was wearing khaki shorts and a lime-green tube top. "Hiya, Henry," she said. It was the first time I'd seen her since I moved in. She was prettier than I remembered.

I angled my bag into the mouth of the dumpster.

"We're painting this thing yellow," Mariana said. "Uncle Dewey thinks this'll make it more attractive to passersby." She looked up and down the alley. "On this thoroughfare here." She balanced her brush across the lip of the can and stood up to shake my hand. "You don't look a lot different. I hear you've been hitting on my sister. You still pretty fast out of the blocks, or what?"

"It was his doing," I said, raising my head toward Nassar. "He set it up. Almost got us killed in the process—he tell you about that?"

"I set up the dinner," he said. "I had nothing to do with the dancing."

Mariana grabbed my arm above the elbow and bent forward in mock conspiracy. "Dancing," she said. "See, that's our secret word. A metaphor or something, see?"

"Got it," I said.

She made a face at Nassar. "He doesn't like things that are too, uh, direct," she said, turning me back toward the

142

apartments. "I'm having a talk with Henry now, O.K.? You go ahead with the yellow."

We went into the courtyard and sat down by the pool. She sat on the edge, dangling her legs into the pale-blue water. I took a chair. "So, Henry," she said, watching her feet distort in the ripples. "You got trouble. Just like old times. Have I got it straight? Your first wife stole your second? Is that it?"

"They got to be friends," I said. "I mean, I don't know that that's it. I've only been out a week."

Mariana rocked her hips and edged backward a little, then lifted her legs out of the water. "So, we're working on tactics right at the moment."

"Right," I said.

Both of us looked at the water for a few minutes. It glittered and shined as breezes got its surface. Mariana sighed and slapped the water with her feet. "What's our worst case?"

"I get a new start."

"Whoopee," she said, turning to look at me over her shoulder.

I grinned. "You busy or anything?"

She laughed and pulled her knees up, putting her feet on the pool ledge. She wiggled her toes. "So, what are you doing to these women? How come they like each other better than they like you? She got up, stretched, then slid her hands into her back pockets. "Don't answer. I know. You need practical advice, my main line."

I got up, too. "I remember. You gave me a lot of practical advice when Clare left. You told me to go get her."

"My John Wayne period. Won't work in the new world." She slapped my stomach with the back of her hand. "First we got to lose a little of this. Then, something about the hair—what is that, a Bruce Dern make-over? And the pants, Henry. It's the eighties, right? We don't have to wear jeans anymore. We can get some regular pants. Maybe a shirt with some kind of color, or pattern, or something—and we can get our things dry-cleaned, you know? Give us a crisp look—there's a lot to do here." She walked in circles around me, pulling at my clothes, poking me with stiff fingers.

"This touching stuff, is this part of the treatment?"

She pinched a section of my shirt. "You're still doing all cotton, right? Right. But—what color is this, anyway?"

"White," I said.

"Just kidding. Just playing around. Actually, you don't look bad at all." She stopped right in front of me and tapped my lips with her finger. "Spread 'em."

"What?" I started backing away from her.

She came after me, matching my steps, laughing and clicking one of her long, clear fingernails on her front teeth. "Gums," she said. "Open up. Open up."

We went to the mall, the fish market, then some place across town that was having a sale on French shoes. She told me that she'd talked to Winnie and that Winnie thought I was interesting. I told her about the stupid thing I'd done on Winnie's Answerphone. As we were leaving the shoe store a deafmute guy came up selling ballpoint pens. I gave him a dollar and got a red pen with a small flag attached to its clip.

Mariana said, "There's your problem right there, Henry. Couldn't be more clear."

I watched the guy go down the sidewalk toward the A&P. "You don't want to make too much of it."

"Question of style. You're a born pussy."

"I'm gonna pussy you. You want me to get the dollar back? I'll do it." I turned around and took a couple of steps toward the guy with the pens.

"Eek, eek," she said, putting her hands on her hips. She gave me her bored-to-death look and then spun around and started for the car.

I followed her across the faded blacktop. "I wanted to go through with it, to get my dollar back from the pen guy," I said, getting into the car. "But I didn't."

"We noticed that. They got you coming and going, don't they?"

"Who?"

"Never mind. Forget it." She reached across and knocked on the dashboard in front of me. "Hand me that pistol out of the glove box, will you?"

"You've got a gun in here? I released the latch and peered into the compartment. There wasn't any pistol.

"Just kidding," she said.

I rolled my eyes, but she wasn't looking, she was backing the car out of its slot, so I waited until she turned around, and I rolled my eyes again.

"Saw it the first time," she said. "Why don't you just take it easy here awhile, huh? Kind of ride along, enjoy the scenery—you know, relax. I don't think you're doing so bad. I mean, you could've lost an arm, somebody could've been killed, big shootout over to the One Hour, you know what I mean? You could've been caught with that little Twinkie that's hanging around with your daughter all the time—"

"Her name's Kelsey and she's twenty if she's a day," I said. "Besides, I never touched her."

"There it is again," Mariana said, taking her hands off the wheel and holding them up, palms forward, in front of her. "Maybe you ought to jump her? Show her who's boss. Show the wife. Everybody's doing it."

"Tried that," I said. I fished through the glove compartment and found a Saint Christopher medal that I brought out to look at. Mariana stopped too close to a traffic light and had to lean forward to see it out of the windshield. "So, can we change the subject now?"

She grinned and slapped me on the thigh. "We're just getting started. Bucko. We've got restless nights in the apartment. One after another in a long endless parade—get that? Long and endless, both of those. We got daytime in the kitchen with four red plastic pebble-finish glasses that you bought because they seemed sensible. We got light in there looks like it's trying to kill you. It's ordinary light, coming in windows and stuff, but it's so dusty and dry it's gonna soak you right up off the face of the planet."

She switched lanes very quickly, slipping in front of a mustard-colored BMW.

"So then you put on the radio and what comes out is high school, real soft and sexy. You get a lot of cupped-up breasts in your mind, and that's no good, so you put on a record. You switch on the lights just to get some red into the room. But the record is old and reminds you of something, or it's new, and hip, and you bought it at Eckerd's drugstore."

"But I've got the light going," I said.

"The light's no better," she said. "You burn up the TV trying to get some color into the place, but nothing works. It's a desert in there. You're a thousand miles away, like the song. You ache. You get a woman in and she smells funny. I mean, she doesn't really smell funny, she just smells funny to you. You tell her that and she gets mad."

I pointed to the speedometer. "We've got a thirty-mile zone here."

She pulled off the accelerator and let the car coast until the orange pointer got down to forty.

"So this woman packs up and leaves in a hurry. The apartment looks like the inside of a Bake-O-Matic enamel shop at full tilt and you're in the bedroom with this smell in the sheets and the light looking medical, and you got in your head this picture of a sweet-smelling girl you danced with about twenty years ago on the lawn of a rich kid's house. It's a misty night, fall—cold and sparkly with the patio lights putting tree-trunk shadows across the grass— and this soft girl is up close, her mouth in your neck, and she says something, or you think she says something, so you ask her What? and she rocks her head back and forth, pulling her lips up over the lobe of your ear, and says Uh-huh in a voice that feels like a little warm water going down your legs—"

I put a hand over Mariana's mouth. "I get the picture."
She struggled playfully, then slumped forward onto the
wheel. The car veered off to one side, narrowly missing a
blue mailbox that seemed to come out of nowhere. Mariana
spun the wheel, yelled a muffled "Jesus," elbowed my hand
off her mouth, and sat up, all at once. "Don't mess with
the driver," she said, when we were going smoothly again.
"Sorry," I said. "I had to stop you."
"Stop me what?" I was dramatizing your plight. I was
working." She looked at me and I looked at the car's head-
liner. "So what are you telling me, that you don't want to
go back?"
I rolled down my window and adjusted the outside rearview mirror. "Not a useful question," I said, closing my
window again.
"Yeah, yeah, yeah. You want to answer anyway?"
Her blouse had come unbuttoned. I could see the curve
of the bottom of her breast and the line above it where her
tan cut across the pale skin.
She caught me looking and buttoned her shirt with one
hand. "So, what's the answer, Henry?"
"Don't know," I said.
She nodded and pushed the hair up and away from her
forehead. "I thought so. All the men say that. The women
don't say that at all, see, that's the thing."
I shook my head.
"Sure it is," she said. "You got girls flying away in droves,
caterwauling—going away fast, as if shot from guns." She
illustrated by wagging her hands in circles and then batting
them into each other. "Love doesn't know your name. You've
got a serious problem here, and you're thinking levelhead-
ed's gonna get it." She turned to inspect a guy who had
pulled up alongside us at the light in a GMC truck. I
watched him realize she was looking him over. He was
rubbing his neck, and, when he saw her, he raised his
eyebrows a fraction and, at the same time, dropped his head,
acknowledging her attention.

I don't know what kind of look she gave the guy, but after he'd done his hello there was a pause, then a smile spread slowly over his face. He looked away, then back to her, then past her to me, then at her again. His smile turned into a chuckle.

"He's about a two," Mariana said, still looking at the guy.

"You'd better quit or he'll run that truck up on the back of here and start humping," I said. "What are you doing?"

She turned around. "Practicing." She twisted the wheel back and forth. "Where was I?" She started fast after the light changed, to get the jump on the guy in the truck. "Oh, yeah. I was helping you. I was being seductive."

I squinted at her. "That's very flattering," I said, but it didn't sound right, so I said, "That's nice."

"You're welcome," she said.

She propped her elbow on the door and her head on her hand and drove more slowly. I looked out the window at the hamburger places, fried-fish places, barbecue places. An old guy with a bicycle decked out like a five-and-dime wheeled by on our right with one of his two overcoats tied up into a cowl over his head and a small TV strapped with duct tape to the handlebars of his bike. I reached over and touched Mariana's shoulder.

She shrugged my hand off and then laughed, a lovely short laugh that flickered over her face and ended in a small tight smile for me.

——— • ———

A COUPLE OF days later the classified pages of the current *Chronicle of Higher Education* mysteriously appeared under my apartment door. Southern Baptist College had an ad that had been circled with a red felt-tip pen. The ad was for a one-year, non–tenure-track instructorship in biology. I was still looking through the ads when the department chairman called. "I'm Jack Stibert," he said. "Let me introduce myself. I've heard a lot about you from my sister. In fact, she gave me this number. I hope you don't mind me calling."

"No," I said. "Who's your sister?"

"Mariana Nassar," he said. "You live in one of her apartments, I believe."

I said that I did. We talked for a few minutes and then he invited me to come out and interview for the job that was advertised in the *Chronicle*. "You've seen our ad? Mariana said you'd have it in hand by this morning."

I made some excuses at first, out of nervousness, and because it was such a peculiar situation, but he insisted, so I agreed to drive out there the next morning. "We don't stand on ceremony," he told me. "Call me back if you have any questions."

I tried to call Mariana right away, but no one answered her phone. Then I got a drink out of the refrigerator and tried to think who else I might report this news to. Finally, I dialed the house. Rachel answered. "Why aren't you in school? I asked.

"It's a holiday. What's your excuse?"

I told her about the interview and she said, "Oh, Dad. Why don't you just settle down?"

"Inappropriate response, Rachel," I said.

"I'm sorry," she said. "I guess it's an honor or something, huh? I thought you liked the stuff you were doing."

"Nobody ever called me up out of the blue and asked me to come interview," I said. "It opens up possibilities," I said.

"Uh-huh," she said.

I finished with her and called Roger Hoffman at my office. I told him I wouldn't be in for the next couple of days. He told me everybody knew I was having a personal crisis, so he didn't think there would be a flap. I said I'd missed a lot of work but that it could be figured as sick leave.

"Sure," he said. "Just get well, Henry."

"You bet," I said, after I'd hung up the phone. I was going to go over and leave a note for Mariana to call me, but when I started outside I saw Nassar sitting in one of the metal chairs alongside the pool. It was raining a little and he was just sitting there, staring at the pool. I decided to stay in. I called Rachel again. "I'm going tomorrow," I said. "You can tell Theo if you want to."

"Tomorrow's Wednesday," she said. "O.K. I'll tell her."

I spent the rest of the day working over my vita and trying to call Mariana on the telephone. Twice I hung up on Nassar without saying a word. Late in the afternoon I walked over to Joel's apartment to see if he'd come home yet, but he didn't answer my knock and there was no sign of his being back. At midnight I drove to the all-night drugstore to get a new pair of black socks.

The meeting with the Jack Stibert went well enough. He was younger than me. After lunch he took me to meet the dean of the college, two vice-presidents, and the president, then sat me down in the department lounge. "We like our people to have a chance to meet you on an informal basis," he told me. "Come by my office when you're through."

I met a woman named Donna, an associate professor

from Kansas who said she had a book contract with Plinth and was ready for promotion, and a young guy named Ed Western, who had a consuming interest in the United States Football League. About four-thirty I went around to Stibert's office. He wasn't there, but Mariana was.

"Hello, applicant. How do you like it? Chairman Jack being nice to you?"

"I tried to call you yesterday," I said, sitting on the couch alongside her. "You weren't home."

"Been busy. Fixing you up is tough work. Even for a killer like me. We've got to get Jack for dinner, so don't go all comfortable and laid back on me."

The three of us went to a restaurant called Dreamland that was out in the woods someplace, and when we came back into town the rain that had been on and off had let up. Everything was shiny and bright—the pavement, the stoplights, the violet and green neon from shop windows that lined the street we were on.

"I've had enough school for a lifetime," Mariana said as we drove past the university. "I feel like I've been eating chromosomes here for the last couple of hours. Let's get us some beer, what do you say?"

"I guess so," I said.

"He's insecure," Stibert said, glancing at me in the rear-view mirror. He looked smaller than he was because he was driving Mariana's big car. His hair was springy, red like hers, and floated around the sides of his head.

When we pulled into a 7-Eleven parking lot alongside a police car Mariana said, "Yum yum," pointing to the cop who was inside drinking coffee out of a polka-dot cup. He was a young guy with a little-boy haircut and a black leather jacket, and he had his hat cocked back on his head. "Oh," she said. "It's Burt."

Stibert lifted up in the seat as he reached into his back pocket for his wallet. "Burt's a friend of hers," he said to me.

"Look at him," she said. "He's pudding."

"She really needs a boyfriend," Stibert said, looking at me over his shoulder.

"My brother thinks I'm a one-woman sexual revolution," she said. "He hasn't heard that boys and girls can just be friends." She went inside and got two six-packs of Coors out of the cooler. Then she said something to Burt. They talked while the skinny girl in the red jumper covered with 7-Eleven patches worked the register.

"I kid her," Stibert said. "But she's all right. You have a family?"

I slid down on the back seat and stuck my hand out the open car window to feel the rain. "Four brothers and two ex-wives. And about half a daughter."

"We have a brother in Kansas but we never talk to him. And we have Dewey. You know Dewey, don't you?" He leaned over the seat back. "What are you doing back here?"

"I know him," I said.

"Oh. Right. You live at the apartments."

Mariana and the policeman came out of the store together, still talking. He walked her to the car and opened the door. The interior light came on, and Mariana said, "Meet Patrolman Burt. This is Jack, and that's Henry in back. Jack's my brother."

"Howdy," the guy said. He was bent at the waist so he could see into the car. His jacket creaked.

"He's off duty," Mariana said. "We're going to drive around awhile. I love police cars. Will you come by later?"

"Come by where?" I said.

"We could go to Blister's," Stibert said. "First, I mean."

"Good idea," Mariana said, smiling. "Then, Henry, I'll tell you what Chairman Jack really thinks, O.K.?"

"Maybe I'll tell him myself," Stibert said.

Burt adjusted his gun belt, and, while he wasn't looking, Stibert and Mariana made faces at each other. Then she dropped the sack on the passenger seat.

"An hour?" Stibert said. "You figure to get your driving done by then?"

Mariana turned to me. "Are you all right, Henry?" She sighed and gave me an impatient look. "Oh, get up here in front, will you?" she said, slapping the back of the seat with her palm.

We left Mariana and Burt in the parking lot and drove to Blister's, a college bar full of students and young faculty types. The music was loud. Everyone seemed to be having a good time. Two women signaled Stibert from a table near the bandstand, and when we got to where they were they both started talking right away, completing each other's sentences. The room was dark. The waitresses wore smart yellow tights. I took a seat at one end of the table and said hello to a kid with sideburns, glasses, and a black T-shirt that had COBOL block-lettered across the chest.

Stibert put a hand on my shoulder. "This is Henry." He pointed at the woman next to him. "That's Carmen," he said. "Carmen, you have to do your friends."

"I already did my friends," Carmen said, and everybody laughed. Then she pointed at the people around the table. "This is Mitch. He's art department, so you don't sweat him. I'm Carmen. The guy next to you is Hacker. That's Mamie, and this one"—she patted the head of the woman sitting next to her—"this one with the blue hair is Lucy."

"Hello, Lucy," I said. Lucy had bright eyes to match her hair, which was brushed back and up in a rooster cut.

"Her name's not really Lucy," Carmen said. "Everybody just calls her that."

"Right," Lucy said. "My real name's Alma." Mitch leaned across the table and kissed her on the neck, just inside the collar of her shirt. "A territorial thing," she said, stroking the back of his head.

The waitress brushed her hip against me. I ordered a beer and then listened to two of the women talk about a guy both had had in class. Mitch sat down and put an arm around Stibert. Hacker rubbed his nose in tight circles with his knuckle. "I hear you're interviewing. How'd you do?"

"All right, I guess." I wiggled my beer bottle. "The president had some trouble remembering what I was here for. Outside of that it was fine."

"He has trouble remembering what *he's* here for," Hacker said.

"Laughs?" Carmen said.

"You leave the president alone," Lucy said. "He's all right. So what if he likes plaid?"

"Are you in the biology department?" I asked her.

"Poetry," she said. "I teach poetry and comp. Mamie's in social work, and Carmen—what do you do, Carmen?"

"I show the little coeds how to eat up men."

"I think she means phys-ed," Lucy said. "How come you're with Stibert? Where's Mariana?"

"She's probably doing research," Carmen said. "She does more research than anybody I know."

"Take a hike, Carmen," Mamie said.

"Carmen doesn't really know Mariana," Lucy said, bending the edge of a beer coaster. "Carmen thinks Mariana shouldn't hang around the college. It's a big crime, in Carmen's view. Also, it's competition."

"At least I don't envy her," Carmen said.

Carmen and Mamie got up to dance to a new song on the jukebox, taking Mitch and Hacker with them. Stibert came around to my side of the table and sat next to Lucy. We watched the customers trot out onto the tiny dance floor. A willowy blond guy in a tight emerald muscle shirt and baggy white pants started dancing alone, his eyes closed. The other dancers pulled back to allow him room.

"Who's this?" I asked, bumping Lucy's arm.

"Paul. He tried to hang himself on the high board at the pool. There wasn't any water in the pool. He used an electrical cord, one of those big orange jobs they sell at grocery stores. Some swimming coach got him down."

"Paul's very intense," I said, watching him dance.

"Sure he is," Lucy said, glancing at me and then the Schlitz clock over the bar. "Everybody says that."

We spent an hour at the bar, and when we got outside the rain had started up again. In the car, Stibert told me Mitch was a computer whiz who did statistical studies for the department. "He was Mariana's boyfriend when she got back from Rhodesia. You hear about her trip to Rhodesia?"

"No, I didn't. There's a lot I don't hear about Mariana."

"You're finding out, though. Right?"

"Piecing it together," I said.

We went to an apartment complex called Palm Shadows North. Stibert told me that Mariana owned the apartments, which were Tudor—dark-brown wood crisscrossing stucco buildings that were bathed in white light. When we got into the central yard he pointed at a group of buildings partly hidden by a Japanese rain tree. "Her light's on."

The living room looked like one of those model rooms they always do in department stores. There was a humpback sofa with a matching chair, a giant red Oriental urn, a rattan basket with tall dried weeds inside.

Mariana and Burt were in the kitchen.

"Still warm," Burt said, pointing to a pile of french fries on the counter. He was big, thick through the chest and shapeless from the shoulders down, and young. The tail of his blue police shirt was out, and his black belt was slung over the back of one of the barstools. He stuck out an arm to shake hands. "Burt," he said. "You're Henry, right?"

"He prefers Henry," Stibert said.

Mariana kept pushing the french fries around in a hat-size pot of cooking oil.

"Henry," Burt said, repeating himself uncertainly as he shook my hand.

"Either one." I grinned at him. "Doesn't matter."

"We got tired of driving," Burt said, gripping my shoulder and turning me toward the counter. "We thought we'd make some homemade french fries."

"The first ones burned," Mariana said. "I don't know what I did wrong."

"I told her it was her oil," Burt said. He came up in back of Mariana and patted her rump. She jumped and gave him a look. "Oops," he said. "I think I'd better get the beer. Where's that beer you got?"

I offered to go out to the car, but Burt said he wanted to, and took the keys from Stibert. "Which way is it again?" he said from the apartment door. "Out this way?" He pointed off in the wrong direction.

"Straight across the courtyard and make a right past the mailboxes," Stibert said. "In the first row about twenty down."

"Back in a flash," Burt said.

Stibert leaned against the counter, staring at Mariana, but she ignored him. "Hi, Henry," she said. "You doing O.K.?"

"Fine. I met the faculty."

"The regulars," Stibert said. "So what about Burt?"

"Burt's a vet," Mariana said. "Post-Vietnam. But he learned a whole lot about human nature in the service. He builds model trains. He likes bicycling and he's not good in bed."

"Oh, Jesus," Stibert said. "Is he married or what?"

"His wife was Rose Queen in his high-school pageant. No kids. He says she's O.K."

"Is this peanut oil or regular oil?" I said.

"Crisco," Mariana said. She removed newly browned french fries and rolled them onto paper towels on the counter top. "Salt those, will you?" she said to Stibert.

"Just curious," I said.

Mariana patted my arm. "It's a game we play. Actually, I have no idea about his wife, not to mention how he is in bed. Chairman Jack, however, likes to think of me as a lady of darkness. I do the best I can."

"That's cute," Stibert said. "Poor kid's probably steaming by now."

"He's doing fine," she said. "Anyway, what about that Puerto Rican girl you liked so much? What was her name, Felicidad?"

Burt opened the front door and shouted, "Beer run." He came into the kitchen carrying the sack with the top rolled over like the top of a lunch bag. His shirt was patterned with coaster-size spots. "I sat in the car a minute waiting for the rain to quit. Then I listened to it on the roof—you know, that old car, the way old cars smell, and here's this rain, thunk, thunk, thunk, you know? It's dark. Nobody's around. So I sit there for a minute, just listening. You know what I'm saying?" He put the bag on the counter and unrolled the top. "Maybe not. Who's thirsty?"

"I'll have one," Stibert said, pulling a can out of a six-pack.

"Take off the shirt," Mariana said. "We'll put it back in the oven."

"I'm O.K.," Burt said. He flapped the tail of his shirt. "It'll dry quick enough."

"Oh, go ahead," Stibert said.

Burt shook his head. "Nope." He handed out beer.

Stibert took a Kleenex out of the dispenser on top of the refrigerator and wiped off the top of his Coors can, bunching the tissue to clean the can's rim, then put the beer on the counter and wadded the tissue into a ball, rolling it between his palms.

We drank the beer standing in the kitchen. Stibert kept looking at me as if I was supposed to do something. Finally he said, "We still have to get your car out at the school, right?" He pushed off his stool, drained his beer, then flattened the can on the counter. "Right. It's getting late. Time to move."

"It's only ten o'clock, Jack," Mariana said. She fluffed his hair.

"Class at eight," he said. "I used to like early classes, but

I sure hate the shit out of 'em now."

Burt stuffed his shirttail back into his trousers, wrapped the gun belt around his waist, and put his cap on his head, the visor low over his eyes. "I've got to go," he said.

We went to the door together, the four of us. Burt was the first outside. "Looks like it's quit again," he said, holding his hands out at his sides.

Mariana followed him out and wrapped her arms around his neck. "Thanks, Burt," she said. "I had fun. Really." Without releasing Burt she gave Stibert a high five as he walked past. "So long, Brother." Then she whispered something else to Burt and let him go. I started to follow the other two, but Mariana said, "Wait a bit," and tugged my coat. Stibert and Burt were fifteen feet away, both turned in our direction.

"You coming, Henry?" Stibert said.

Burt adjusted his cap, then put his hands on his hips, staring at Mariana, then at me. He was still for a minute, then abruptly turned, waving over his shoulder. "Night," he said.

"Meet you at the car?" Stibert said.

"Take yours," Mariana said. "I'll run him home."

"He's got to get his car," Stibert said. He caught Burt halfway across the courtyard, and by the time they made the turn to go past the mailboxes they were laughing. The sound echoed in the yard, which was full of lights bouncing off the wide blades of the yuccas, off the wet bushes. Everywhere there was the sound of dripping water. Mariana put an arm around my waist and I put an arm around hers and we stood there watching Stibert and Burt.

"I like them," she said. "Isn't that strange?"

Mariana took me home, saying we could get the car the next day. She didn't say a word about the apartment or the cop. We talked about the job, and me taking the job, and about her brother whom she swore she'd told me about a hundred times. I was sure I'd never heard of him.

* * *

I met her in the courtyard at eleven-thirty the next morning. It wasn't raining, but the sky was dark and there was an occasional rumble of thunder off in the distance. She had to stop at the bank on our way to college. When we got in line for the Autoteller she bumped into the back of a Dodge Polaris. "How about we get some lunch first?" she said, watching the driver in front look at who'd hit him.

"How about we get some insurance?" I said.

"I guess you want to know what's going on, huh? Crazy housewife and all that. Well, Dewey's used to me. It's an arrangement we have. I don't do it nearly as much as I used to, and he doesn't mind, or not much. He thinks it's O.K. We don't talk about it anymore."

"It's interesting," I said.

"That it works? Yeah, I guess so." She took me to a restaurant called Seafood in the Rough, where the drinks came in glasses shaped like telescopes. She looked at the menu and decided on crab claws.

"Do they fry chicken and fish in the same oil?" I said.

She called the waiter over and asked about the chicken. He was eighteen and looked like John Travolta, with the wet eyes and the jaw. He liked the trout, only they were out of trout. He was mixed on the chicken and didn't know anything about the oil.

I said, "I thought it was traditional in a place like this."

"No kidding?" he said.

Mariana ordered for both of us and asked him to send the cocktail waitress back. "After lunch I want to show you Jack's apartment. You'll be amazed, O.K.?"

The chicken was served with garlic toast and a bowl of cold peanut butter and honey, a thick paste, that Mariana said was wonderful. I was skeptical, but tried it anyway, and she was right. We asked the waiter about the peanut butter and honey and he didn't know anything about it. "It's just what they do here," he said. "It may be Samoan."

"It's my treat," Mariana said, when the bill came.

Stibert's place was a couple of two-bedroom townhouse apartments converted into one, and it smelled like cinnamon and had a lot of furniture. Everything was jumbled together. There was a coffee table with a glass top that covered an Indian sand painting, and there were oil paintings of horses—horses standing alongside red-jacketed girls, horses staring into the cramped rooms, horses with blue ribbons pinned to them. At one end of the living room there were two sliding doors covered with satiny curtains that almost glowed. Low, shaded lamps provided a brownish light. I made a face by way of appreciation, and Mariana said, "You like it, right?"

"It's pretty mysterious," I said.

She tugged on the curtain so she could look outside. There was a flash of lightning and she jumped away from the window. "It's great out there," she said.

I looked at a brass pot stacked with some other pots next to the wall, then settled on the floor and leaned against the couch. "I don't think I slept enough last night. What time did we get home?"

She stopped right in front of me, close, for a minute, and flicked my hair around with her hand. "Oh, it was terribly late, maybe eleven-thirty. You like night, you told me." I stared at where her knees were under the skirt, then looked at her shoes, which were almond-colored with open toes and high heels. The cinnamon smell was strong. I touched her shoe and she took a step closer, then backed away and went into the bedroom. After a few minutes she appeared again wearing a floor-length black silk robe decorated with red piping and a Chinese dragon, antique and stunning. "You want some space candy?" she said, tearing the top of a bag. She flipped her hair out of the collar of the robe. "I'm nuts for the stuff."

"Me too," I said. "What is it?"

She poured some kernels of the candy into my palm. The candy looked like small gray rocks. "Put them on your tongue."

I did that and the candy seemed to explode inside my head. "I remember this stuff," I said. "Some friend of Rachel's gave me some of this in the grocery store once."

"Kids used to have this all the time. I think it had to be taken off the market or something. Jack's got cases and cases."

She went across the room to a lacquered dressing table that was built around a huge round mirror. She sat with her back perfectly straight and studied her makeup, and when she combed her hair she did it the way women do in shampoo commercials, dreamily, as if the hair were precious. She was watching me watch her in the mirror. Finally, she slid the comb into a drawer, swiveled around, and dropped the robe off her shoulders. She made a little flourish with her hands.

I said, "Yikes."

"Yikes?" She raised an eyebrow at me and then, when I didn't move, she turned and looked at herself, brushed her fingers across her breasts, and bent down for the robe, which she folded over her hands in her lap.

"Just something that came to mind," I said. "You're real pretty."

"Thanks." She waited another minute, then shook the robe out and started to put it on. "My idea of a friendly gesture," she said.

I got off the floor and went over to her and we looked at each other in the mirror. "Can we get to this point again?" I said.

She laughed and said, "Sure. So, you want to go to a movie or something?"

"What a wonderful idea," I said.

She slid to one side of the stool so I could sit down and then she put her head on my shoulder, then kissed my arm, leaving a pair of shiny red lips on my shirtsleeve.

* * *

She dropped me off at the college. I drove around for a while, hitting a lot of streets I'd never seen before. Finally I pulled into the parking lot of a motel called the Tropic Breeze. It was a fifties place with a fresh coat of aquamarine paint and the trim done in coral.

I sat in the car for half an hour, watching the street and the registration desk and the customers. Some guy I guessed was the manager noticed me sitting in his parking lot and he kept coming out of the glassed-in lobby every four or five minutes. I decided I ought to go for a walk. The motel was on a street lined with fast-food restaurants and gas stations, so I didn't go far. It was cool and there were breezes, quick bursts that bent tree limbs and rattled signs. There was a big live oak in among the buildings, next to an abandoned Roy Rogers Roast Beef place, and in it there was a platform treehouse with three low walls made out of auto hubcaps. The cars going by had their parking lights on, their tires hissing on the dark pavement. A red pickup went by and the driver honked. I waved even though I didn't know who it was—it could've been somebody I knew, or somebody who thought I was somebody else. I sat down on a concrete bench at the bus stop and watched the cars.

It was close to six when I got home. Mariana was leaning on the metal railing outside my apartment wearing an ice-blue leotard, a leather flight jacket with a fur collar, and a pair of bulky silver pants like some I'd seen in *TV Guide*.

"I'm early," she said, as I climbed the stairs.

"I'm lucky," I said.

"I've been working out," she said, showing me the weights she had in each hand. "I always carry these things around." She did a couple of demonstration curls, first one hand and then the other, her breasts popping under thin fabric. "This place looks like a golf course. I've never understood why he does this." She lifted her head to indicate the courtyard.

"I like it," I said.

She held the dumbbells over her head and then slowly lowered her arms until they were fully extended straight out from her shoulders. "You lift?"

Nassar came out of their apartment wearing caramel-and-white saddle oxfords, a white undershirt, and high white pants with a thin cordovan belt that seemed to be twisted in the loops. He looked as if he'd just shaved—his skin was smooth and sunburn red. He had moles that looked like erasers on his shoulders. "What's this?" he said. He looked at me, then licked his finger and tapped it on the burning tip of his cigar.

"This is Henry improvement," Mariana said. She dropped the weights onto the balcony. "We're also talking about getting you a rocket ship for your place here."

He looked at the grounds. "I've been thinking about a giraffe," he said. "Real tall guy." He looked again, sighed, got the newspaper from the flower bed by the door, and went inside.

"He likes you," I said.

She pinched the lapel of my jacket and tugged. "C'mon. I'm a knockout with a strange apartment."

I unlocked the door and we went in.

"How come there's no furniture? What's he doing in here? Is open plan making a comeback?" The apartment hadn't seemed strange to me until she came in and started looking at it. I followed her around, into the kitchen, then the bedroom. "Maybe you should get some spotlights in here," she said. "So where were you? Did you call me?"

"I went for a walk."

"Smooth. That's the professor in you. Me, I was lonely." She dropped the leather jacket on the floor, then straightened the Danskin over her belly. "I almost hit somebody in a parking lot." She turned to look out the window. "Shut the curtains. So, are you taking the job?" She grinned at me for a minute, then she grabbed a handful of the silver material bunched around her knee. "You ever see these things? They make you look so stupid, but they work. I lost two pounds. I had to send away for them." She pressed the fabric into folds that she traced up and down her thighs. "I go through pants pretty quick, but these dudes are permanent."

M ARIANA AND I took an eighteen-passenger Republic flight to Brownsville, then rented a car at the airport and drove over to Port Isabel, a coast town in extreme south Texas. We went for the weekend. There were palm trees lining the highway. People pulled carts in the dirt alongside the road. Very quaint. Mexico was about twenty-five minutes away. The rain was thick and blue, falling constantly, relentlessly, as it had done since we left home. I had called Rachel to tell her I was going out of town to think things over. Rachel said, "That's what I'm supposed to tell Mom?"

When we got into Port Isabel we dropped our bags in the lobby of the Alamo Hotel and went for a drink at a club called the Tim Tam, which was full of prostitutes. They were dancing together, circling clumsily in dots of light from a fifties beer advertising display. We drank Superior and watched the women dance. Mariana said, "How about this one?" She indicated a woman in a black sheath slit over the hip. "You want us to wrap her for you? Henry?" She fiddled with the thick chips in a gold basket on the table.

"It's to go," I said. "Maybe we should walk around, see the town." I glanced out the yellow saloon-style doors at the rain. "No, I guess we shouldn't."

"We can run to the hotel, if you want."

One of the women we had been staring at, not the one in black, came to the table and leaned on the third chair. She had on elbow-length gloves and a T-shirt with no sleeves. Her nipples were large circles against the shirt. "This your first time?" She glanced around at the little bar, which was dark and used-looking. "Ain't much, is it? Good against rain and not much else. I'm saying we got a perfect roof, though. Tight as a drum." She waved at the ceiling.

"Just taking a look," Mariana said.

"That's what I see. I'm Felice." She winked at me. "I figured you weren't, you know, customers, in the usual sense of that term."

Mariana said, "My name is Mariana. This is Henry. We just got here. For the weekend."

"Uh-huh. And you ain't Texas, are you? I can tell Texas born. Except Houston. Those folks always sound like they're from L.A., or either Michigan. One of the two."

I said, "We're at the hotel a couple of blocks over here." I pointed toward where I thought the hotel was.

"Are you, now." Felice said. "The Alamo. I've been in there. Seen some of my better days there, matter of fact. You kids having another beer?"

We thanked her and said no, and she thanked us and said to keep her in mind, businesswise. We said that we would, and then all three of us laughed.

The hotel was a six-story brick building on a square that opened on its fourth side to a seedy little dock where people got boat rides. The trees in the square were tall, but they had thin trunks. The man behind the hotel desk was Hawkins, a cripple with a built-up black shoe on his left foot, and a back about twenty degrees off the vertical. We had used Mariana's card to register, so he called me Mr. Nassar.

Alongside the desk a sleepy-looking girl about twenty was shaking a clear plastic rain hat. She said, "Sweet Jesus. He's really after me this time."

"Who is?" Hawkins was staring at the wall of slots behind the desk, trying to find our key.

The girl grinned at Mariana, then at me. "Him," she said, pointing up. "Big Guy. It ain't rained like this since I was a kid in love with Rodney Beauchamp. I did naughty things for Rodney Beauchamp in his pickup—he was the football captain at my school. The Big Guy rained on me nearly a month. On that occasion."

Hawkins introduced us. "This is Mr. and Mrs. Nassar. Mariana and—is it Henry? Henry. Meredith Rotel. Meredith does the night work on the desk here. She's a local girl."

"Eighty percent local," Meredith said. "The rest of me's entirely rayon."

I signaled hello, and Mariana stepped around toward the side of the desk to shake the girl's hand.

Hawkins wiggled his head back and forth as if to dismiss Meredith's remark. "She'll run you ragged if you give her a chance. Won't you, Meredith? Don't ask her about hot spots, whatever you do."

"I'm the hottest spot I know," Meredith said. She flapped the collar of her print shirtwaist. "Only at the moment I ain't so hot. More wet, like."

"Well, I guess we'll be talking to you," Mariana said, grinning at the girl. "I want to hear more about the pickup."

"Me too," I said.

Mariana slapped my chest. "Settle down there, Big Guy."

We got the key and squeezed into the elevator. The trim was brass and badly stained and there was some kind of Astroturf on the walls. We got off on the third floor and found our room, which was large and sour-smelling, with two windows overlooking the square. I took a chair by one of the windows and cocked my feet up on the radiator.

Mariana sat on the bed. "We shouldn't have gone to the bar first thing. Right? So, I think what I'll do is shower and take it easy for a bit." She unbuttoned the front of her blouse, then its cuffs. She pulled her suitcase onto the bed and popped it open, bringing out a plain leather travel kit. She loosened her belt, then stood by the bathroom door, one hand on the frame. "Well," she said, straightening her blouse with her free hand. "We could just forget it if that's what you want. I think it'll get better, but it's no big deal."

"It's a fair-size deal, isn't it? It's not routine—maybe for you, not me."

"Oh, heck yes," she said, turning away, entering the bathroom. "I come here all the time. I always come here. I was here last week with this guy who plays pro hockey."

"Sorry," I said.

She looked back into the room and waved off the apology, then closed the door.

I sat in the chair and scanned the square, listening to the water sizzling in the bathroom. Somebody knocked at the door. I answered and a guy in a khaki uniform introduced himself—C.E. "Butch" Corbett, sheriff of Olympia County. He was six-five, easily. I nodded at his badge and then invited him in, but he stayed in the hall. "You Joseph Butcher?" he said.

I said I wasn't. When he asked for identification I gave him my wallet. "Vacation?" he said. "Or business?"

"We're having a small vacation. Just a weekend."

He was like a giant William Bendix, with the slablike jaw and the limp mouth. He glanced up and down the corridor. "You met any people here, staying here?"

"We met the desk guy and a girl who works nights, Meredith. That's all."

He handed me my wallet and stuck his hands in his jacket pockets. "Fine. Thanks. Sorry to bust in."

I said, "I wish I could help you," then waited for him to move away from the door before I closed it, only he didn't move. "Is there something else?" I asked.

"Nope. You can go ahead and shut her down. We appreciate your cooperation."

He smiled but didn't move. It was awkward closing the door in his face, but there wasn't anything else to do, so I did. When it was shut, I locked it and stood there, listening. For a minute I heard nothing, then I heard his boots shuffle away and then the sound of his knock next door.

Mariana stuck her head out of the bathroom. "Who was that?"

I was still facing the door, bent forward. "He said he was the sheriff. I sure was glad to see him, too. I'm just glad I'm not Tuesday Weld or I'd be in real trouble right about now." I went back to my chair. "How did we dig up this place?"

She stepped into the room with a hotel towel pressed against her chest. "Sheriff? I don't believe you."

"He had a badge and everything. I checked it out. I was tough on him, studied the badge. It was a star on something that looked like a horseshoe—it wasn't a horseshoe, but it was shaped like that." I drew the shape in the air. "It had those balls on the star points."

"So he wouldn't hurt himself." She lifted her wet hair, pushed it back above her ear.

"Well," I said, slapping the arm of the chair and then standing. "I'm ready for the big checkout. Find a Holiday Inn or something. Down by the beach—which way is the beach? Over here?" I pointed toward the square.

"Don't be silly. Just because a local peace officer pays us a visit?" She made a face and came across the room.

"He gave me the willies," I said.

"I'm going to give you the willies," Mariana said. "After a while. Right now I'm getting dressed."

When she was ready we went out hunting for a restaurant. Meredith suggested Motor Bill's, a seafood house two or three blocks away, along the harbor. "It's my type of a place," she said. "Kind of a more natural atmosphere."

It was a pretty evening. There were people in the street even though it was still sprinkling. They were walking in twos and threes, enjoying themselves. The sky was a breathtaking silver. We were about half a block from the hotel when the square suddenly filled up with police cars. They slid around corners and out of alleys, without sirens, engines sounding like wind as they accelerated, then stopped hard and diagonal in the street, their top lights flicking the buildings with reds and blues. People started gathering in a circle around the Alamo's entrance canopy. The streetlamps were already on, dropping freezing green circles of light on the pavement. Across the small square, pleasure boats pulled dully at their ropes.

We went back and joined the people in front of the hotel. I heard someone say that somebody was the daughter of a Latin who ran the largest rancho in Panama. Two other guys were talking about a business deal, and the first said, "Hey, the deal is cut, I'm just down here for the signature," and the second said, "Sure you are. And they're talking about sending you to Cairo. That must be swell."

The cops stayed a couple hundred yards away on either side of the hotel, next to their cars, lights still swiveling, flashing. They seemed less concerned with us than with the park and the street. We were in a circle, but there wasn't anything at the center, so I guessed we were waiting on somebody. I said to a small man in a gray chalk-stripe suit, "What's the story?"

The guy turned and looked at me, then at Mariana. I put my arm around her. He said, "Out of town?"

"Right," I said. "What's this about?"

"Nothing for you to worry," he said. His tie had a gold clip in the shape of a musical note about three-quarters of the way down. He fingered the clip as he talked to us. "It's a local situation. You're visiting, so you've got no worry." He got a business card from his vest pocket and handed the card to Mariana. "I am Muhal Richard Cisco. Export. If I can help, please call me. Don't hesitate."

I peeked over Mariana's shoulder at the card, which had on it his name and a ten-digit phone number. Nothing else. Then a tall Mexican guy whispered something to Cisco, who eyed us as he listened, nodding and patting the tall guy's arm. A squinchy kid in white pants and sparkling red shoes pushed his way through the hotel's revolving door. He stayed close to the building. Several people from the group pressed forward, closing around him. They talked nervously, several at once, until the tall guy who had been with Cisco handed the kid some folding money, a lot of it, and the kid managed a toothy grin and slipped back into the hotel.

Mariana said, "I'm thinking maybe you were right. Shall we go?"

We crossed the square and walked down along the dock until we found the restaurant Meredith had recommended. It was a tiny wood-frame building with a tile floor, bum furniture, and plastic tablecloths decorated with farm animals. We sat in a corner under a hanging jade plant that was on its last leg. Our table butted up against a window that had been painted out, brown, but fist-size spots had been scratched clean, so we could see out on a timber dock that had a couple of white rowboats tied to it. A guy wearing a full-length apron over his undershirt came from the back of the restaurant and said something to the girl who had seated us, then brought over two bond-paper menus sleeved in plastic.

Mariana ordered fried scallops and I said I'd try the snapper. The guy took our menus and disappeared back through the swinging doors, each of which had half a circle of dirty glass in it.

There weren't any other customers. On the opposite wall there was a kind of altar—a black sombrero surrounded with photographs, palm leaves, statues, a rosary made of nuggets of red glass, airplane postcards, other stuff. Mariana got up to take a look. I watched the boats out the scratched brown glass. Coming back, she said, "So, what do you say, Henry?"

"It's sweaty for my taste," I said. "Colorful, but sweaty. We could go out where the rest of the tourists are, wherever that is."

"It's not like I remember it, that's true. Probably just a lottery guy—the kid, I mean."

She slid her jacket off her shoulders onto the spindles of the ladder-back chair. Out the hole I saw the guy in the

apron trot past the boats and around the corner of a rusted
steel shed. I waited for him to come back. When he did,
he was carrying a stack of Styrofoam containers like those
used for takeout food. Two Mexican kids wearing khaki
pants and open shirts ran alongside him, talking and gesturing. I said, "I think Motor Bill just ran out and picked
up dinner."

Mariana leaned across the table to see, but the guy was
out of sight.

The kids were about Rachel's age, maybe a little older.
They came in from the kitchen laughing, then saw us and
got very quiet as they sat down at a wobbly table. The guy
who had taken our order came out and said something in
Spanish to the boys, and they screeched their chairs across
the floor and followed him into the back.

The food was served on colored plates—mine was peach,
Mariana's was lime—and it wasn't bad. She kept telling
me to slow down, that I was eating too fast. Out the window
I saw the Mexican kids running along the pier away from
the restaurant carrying garbage bags twisted down to the size
of footballs. The undershirt guy came out to see how things
were going.

"Very tangy," Mariana said. "I love the butter sauce."

"Thank you," the guy said. "You would like to have a
jar of pulque? I have a pulque that you would never forget
in a thousand years."

"He's going to get us on the flies," I said, half whispering
and half muttering.

The guy heard me and didn't think it was funny. He
swatted at the next table with the dish towel he carried over
his arm, then put on a too-polite smile. "You do not have
to drink the pulque, my friend. I have only offered it to the
lady who you are with. If she does not want the pulque
then I am sure that she will not have it."

"I think I won't, today," Mariana said, smiling at the
guy. She dabbed at the corners of her mouth with her

napkin. "But thank you very much. It's kind of you."

"You are welcome," he said, and he bowed at the waist, giving us a view of the top of his head, where a scab the size of a quarter was tucked in under the damp hair.

When he was gone I apologized. "Uncontrollable urge. The flies, I mean. It was stupid. It just leaped out. I'm covered with embarrassment."

"You're gonna be covered with pulque if you don't settle down."

The guy put a guitar record on an old turntable propped up behind the bar, but the music was hard to listen to because a CB radio cut in and out. Mariana turned around and smiled at the guy anyway.

We finished dinner pretty quick and went back out into the drizzle. Mariana had her hair pulled back tight to her scalp. Drops of the mist settled in the wiry hair above her forehead, making her younger and prettier. She took my arm and steered us down a crooked street lined on either side with buildings painted hot, chalky colors. The cars were parked crazily, in the road and up on the sidewalk. At first we climbed around them, then we gave up and took to the middle of the street. I was watching my feet when the two Mexican kids appeared out of a low doorway and asked us if we wanted to buy vegetables. Very fresh, they assured us.

I was all ready to say no when Mariana said yes. She got out her wallet and gave one kid a five-dollar bill while the second kid ducked back in the doorway and fetched one of the garbage bags I'd seen them with earlier. The bag was green and a little bit transparent, and through it I could make out carrots and round things that might have been peppers or red onions. Mariana took the bag and peered down into it, then grinned at the kids. "Terrific," she said. "Wonderful. Thank you."

They thanked her in Spanish and vanished through a royal-blue door.

We went on walking, arm in arm, along the curving, sloping road. The rain was so light I could barely feel it, but I was still getting cold. "This goes down to the Gulf. That's what we want?"

"I want to play cards in bed tonight," Mariana said. "I love to do that. For starters. It slows everything down."

My heel skidded on a badly set paving block and I would have fallen on my face if she hadn't held me up with her arm. "I'm ready when you are," I said, freeing myself. "I need to get me a pink suit and duck shoes to walk around down here."

Saturday morning I went to the lobby and called Rachel. She didn't sound happy to hear from me. I asked about her mother, and about what was happening, and so on, and her answers were terse—single words. Finally I said, "What's wrong here? What are you mad about?"

"Oh, nothing. Only, where are you? What are you doing there? Who's with you?"

"Texas, nothing, and for me to know," I said. "I'm just taking some time off." Hawkins was about twenty feet away, behind his desk, stealing glances at me.

"You're taking a ride on the Reading, is what you're taking. I suggest you get your story together. What am I supposed to say to Mom?"

"I told her what I was doing," I said.

"Yeah, but she's not dumb about it."

I waited a second, then said, "This is great. I feel lousy, so I call you up and what I get is worse than what I started with. Thanks a lot."

"So jump a plane. I'll set it up for you."

I found a wad of grape-colored gum somebody had stuck to the wooden wing of the telephone enclosure. "I'll be back tomorrow afternoon," I said. "You can take me out to dinner."

"What if I don't want to?" I didn't answer that, and she waited for a minute, then said, "O.K. Sorry. Tell me how big a deal this is. I mean, what's the correct level of anxiety for a child like me?"

"You could probably guess. I'm calling you up in the middle of it. Not high."

"Good." She sighed and her voice softened. "In that case, go ahead and have a really wonderful time."

"Thanks, amigo," I said. We hung up and I sat there for a while, feeling better.

It was still raining when we got the car out of the shedlike garage and drove out to the beach for lunch. Mariana was driving and being quiet. I stared out the window. I liked the desolate, broken-down look of things. The land was empty and, in spite of the rain, stretched miles in all directions. We passed a big, shallow hill that was a field full of wrecked cars, and around the cars there were black-and-white cows grazing, and birds strutting quickly in the rain. I knotted my hands together and grinned at how lovely that was. We made a turn onto a road that was straight and thin to the horizon. The palms that staked either side were a hundred yards apart and forty feet tall, curved by the wind.

Mariana glanced around, then turned back to the highway. "Feeling better?"

"I called home. Rachel wanted to know about you. I didn't tell her."

"Oh. Not feeling better. I see." She changed her position behind the wheel, then curled her fingers around her hair, dragging it away from her face. "Do you want to go back today?"

I watched a truck in the rearview mirror on my side of the car. "No. I don't think so. We've got cards to play. You think I'm letting you get away the big winner?"

"No," she said. "I don't."

She turned and smiled at me, a wry, sad smile that made me long for her and for other things. I started to cry and covered it by looking out the window at the stiff trunks of the trees, and the delicate grass, and the helmetlike sky. The tires ran on the highway, and the windshield wipers clacked, and I waited a minute before I faced Mariana again.

"Easy," she said, reaching to circle her hand around my wrist.

R ACHEL AND Kelsey came over Sunday night. Rachel
gave me a stiff hug about chest high as I let her in
and then, without letting me out of her grasp, started talking
about Theo. "She misses you, Dad. You've got her on the
run. She and Clare had a big fight. I think you ought to
make your move pretty quick."

I patted her head. "Thanks for the tip." I reached to shake
hands with Kelsey.

She kissed my cheek just under and in front of my ear.
"Hi," she whispered. "How's it going?"

Rachel was sort of jammed in between us. "I got the job,"
I said. "If that's what you mean."

"That's what she really means," Rachel said, elbowing
both of us. "Yes, sir. Let's go eat."

Kelsey's car was triple-parked in front of the apartments.
Rachel climbed into the back seat and I got in front. Kelsey
shoved a tape into the dashboard tape player and turned up
the volume.

"It's her favorite song," Rachel said. She was draped over
the backs of the front seats, her chin right next to my shoulder. At the chorus, Kelsey sang along, then Rachel sang
with her. After a couple of minutes I sang, too. Kelsey kept
rewinding the tape. While she was doing that, Rachel and
I tried to get the rest of the words down. Then Kelsey would
start the song over and we'd listen, keeping time, hitting on
the chorus.

We made three or four circles through town trying to
figure out where to eat, then Kelsey wanted to see Southern
Baptist, so we drove out there, then to the motel section,
where the Ramada was. Nobody was hungry, it turned out.

177

Kelsey drove into the old section where Theo and I had bought the house. I tapped her shoulder and wagged my forefinger more or less in her face, but she just grinned. "We're not stopping or anything."

Rachel pushed forward and popped the cassette out of the player. "Where aren't we stopping?" she said to Kelsey.

"Your house. I thought we'd give him a look."

Rachel leaned head and shoulders into the front seat, turning to look at me. "I'd say it's heart trouble if you keep on," she said.

"I'm fine," I said.

Kelsey pulled up at a stop sign and waved impatiently at a low-riding Starfire that was hesitantly turning left from the opposite side of the intersection. "Well?" She elbowed Rachel back into the rear seat.

"Home," Rachel said.

We went back to my apartment. Kelsey said she had errands to run. Rachel wanted to stay. "I can get you about ten," Kelsey said. "Unless I get wrapped up in something."

"She's seeing her boyfriend," Rachel explained to me. "He's this drippy guy with no teeth."

Kelsey walked me toward the door. "I'm worried about this job. I don't want you fooling around with teenagers unless it's me."

I squinted at her and opened the door.

When Kelsey was gone, Rachel got a bottled Coke out of the refrigerator and followed me into the bedroom. I hoisted a box of shirts I'd just gotten back from the laundry onto the bed. "I thought you always got your shirts on hangers," she said.

I put the shirts on the shelf in the closet. "So, what about this fight?"

"They had this argument or something. Clare threatened to move." She gave me her thoughtful look. "Dad? Don't you feel kind of aimless, living over here? By yourself and everything? I mean, I feel aimless since you left, kind of like I'm always wandering around somewhere. Like there's nowhere to go, really." She was on her stomach, with her head over the edge of the bed and her Coke on the floor, poking her forefinger in and out of the bottle's mouth. "It's just kind of weird, you know? Like it's another planet over there or something."

I sat in the bedroom chair that had come with the apartment, an old armchair covered in reddish-brown velour, and looked at Rachel's sneakers, which were bright blue. "I feel O.K.," I said. "It's not much different."

"That's a lie, Dad. Even I know that."

I stared at the arm of the chair. "I mean, what's so different? I'm around, you're around, she's around. We're all around."

"Ugh," she said, crossing her eyes. "Meet Mr. Cosmic." She turned over on the bed and propped herself up on an elbow. "So are you guys getting a divorce or what? I've been thinking about that a lot. I've decided I can handle it. I told Mom already."

"Oh, yeah? What'd she say?"

"She said I shouldn't think about it." Rachel waved a hand at me. "What's wrong with my shoes? Why were you staring at my shoes?"

I went into the kitchen. She came after me, sucking on the Coke bottle, watching me go through the refrigerator, then the cabinets. "They're blue," I said. "I was admiring them." I got down the Raisin Bran.

"That's great, Dad. Thanks. So what are you going to do?"

"None of your business," I said, gently pushing her aside so I could get the milk out of the refrigerator.

"That's an attractive thing to say to your stepdaughter." She pointed her bottle at the milk carton. "I'd smell that before I used it. Do you think I'm too aggressive? I mean, do you like people more when they're shy?"

The milk smelled fine. I said, "This is O.K."

"I'm not shy, but there are some kids at school who are, you know? Everybody likes them."

"And hates you," I said.

"Some of the kids like me, I guess. But Matty Powell says I'm too aggressive to be really well liked. Her parents are divorced."

"Want some cereal?" I said.

"She says I act wrong, like some kind of orphan or something, whatever that means."

"Whatever that means," I said, duplicating her delivery. She took a long drink of her Coke and then shrugged. "The orphan stuff, right?"

"Yep." I dug around in the bowl for the raisins.

"I figured. But, really Dad, why don't you talk to her? Mom, I mean. You guys don't even talk to each other or anything."

"I talked to her. When Cindy was in the hospital. She wasn't friendly, if you know what I mean."

"Things change, Dad."

"Umm," I said.

Kelsey got back at nine-thirty. Joel was with her. He was wearing swimming trunks and a Hawaiian shirt, and he was tanned up. "Well," I said to Rachel. "Looks as if your Uncle Joel and your friend Kelsey have some business together."

"I wish," Joel said. He crossed the living room in four steps and disappeared into the kitchen.

"He was on your stairway," Kelsey said. "He's real sad about something."

"That ain't the word," Joel said from the kitchen. "Clare's going to Colorado." He came out with two cans of beer. "Permanently. I asked her if she wanted me to go and she said no."

Rachel gave me an I-told-you-so look, got one of the beers away from Joel, and took it back into the kitchen. "One at a time," she said.

"You saw her?" I said.

"She's over at my apartment looking for things she left

last time she moved out. She's decided she doesn't want to be gay after all." He wiggled the butt of his can at Rachel, then at Kelsey. "That's not what she said, it's what I said, O.K.? My fault."

"It's fine with me," Rachel said. "We're all adults here."

"That's good, Rachel," I said. "Keep that in."

"My date wasn't so great, if anybody cares," Kelsey said. She'd dropped into the brown sofa. "His sexuality wasn't uncertain, however."

"I think it's interesting," Rachel said. "Whether it's true or not."

Joel drained the beer and went back to the kitchen for the can Rachel had taken away from him. "I was talking about Clare, anyway. I wasn't even thinking of Theo."

"Give us a break here, will you?" I said.

"Mom can take care of herself, Dad," Rachel said.

"Right, Dad," Joel said, coming back into the room. "Took care of you, didn't she?"

"I think I'll go talk to Clare," I said. "You guys are too tough for me."

"You'd better," he said. "We were getting along fine until she found you." He sat down in one of the dining chairs, facing the table, his back to us, and spun his beer can a couple of times. "I should have known when they went out there before," he said. "I should have known when I was sixteen."

"Maybe we'd better move along," Kelsey said. She rolled off the couch and wagged a finger at Rachel. "Let's go, Little Fella. These old guys have work to do."

I walked Rachel and Kelsey out onto the balcony. Rachel hugged me and whispered, "Think about what I said, O.K.? About Mom."

I hugged her and said I would, then nodded at Kelsey, who was already halfway down the metal stairs. "This kid is right," she said. "You're missed over there. A stabilizing influence, know what I mean? Seems incomplete without you."

I waved and watched the two of them clatter down the steps, then stop for a closer look at Nassar's cow, which had a new green light in it, shining up its eyes. I went back inside.

Joel had moved to the couch. "I'm sorry. It's just that I come home and things are ten times worse. I have to take it out on somebody."

I slumped into the chair opposite the couch, folding my hands above my eyes to block the light from a floor lamp.

He twisted his head around to look at me. "So what do I do about Clare? Wait—don't answer. I think we had this conversation already. I remember. It wasn't much help."

"Thanks," I said.

He waved a hand at me. "I was just remembering. No offense."

I listened to the hum of the refrigerator and the occasional muscling of the water pipes, and watched Joel stare at the ceiling. He didn't move, just stared and blinked every four or five seconds. Finally, he took a deep breath, sighed, then pushed up on the couch and sat forward, elbows on his knees, head down. "I'm kind of a slob," he said. "I don't blame her, I guess."

I shut my eyes. "Take it easy," I said.

"Personal crap always wrecks me. There isn't anything to say, you know? That's the trouble. It's so nuts. Like getting run over by a car in slow motion after you've been watching it come at you forever." He sighed again.

"You sound tired," I said.

"No kidding. Clare is going back to the guy she left you for, whatever his name is, and she won't even barely talk to me in the first place because she's been living at your house for a month, hanging out with your wife—I mean, I'm getting used to that idea and here she goes off to some ski resort. And I'm tired? Jesus. It's no wonder you're jacking around out here by yourself."

"It's a good world, isn't it?" I said. "Yep. Dynamic and amazing. And we're part of it, Joel. We're discovering stuff.

Like, that we haven't been paying attention. I mean, we're in a short-yardage situation here, am I right? This is our moment, I'm telling you. This is really something."

"This here is the moronification of girls," he said.

"So they want Richard Gere, so what? Can't have him."

"They're sad about it—a big crisis or something. They sit around in moon faces so we know how hard they're working."

"Yeah. I know—what do they think we're doing? Forget it. Let's see how Clare is. She probably needs a ride."

"I owe her that, right? I'll be polite and she'll be terse—I've done a hundred of those."

"Me too," I said.

He balanced a crumpled beer can on the sofa arm. "I mean, I just want her to stay. If I could get it cheating, I would."

I stuck my hand out to help him up off the couch. He looked at it for a minute, then looked at my face. Just as I started to pull my hand back he put his out.

"O.K.," he said, getting up. "Maybe we can go to a movie or something. I don't know."

"Sure," I said. "We'll show 'em."

We were still shaking hands when Clare knocked on the door, then let herself in. "I've been watching you," she said. "You look like a couple of fruitcakes in here."

Joel laughed too much. I said, "We're working up male bonding."

"Funny, Henry." She did the shortest tour yet of the apartment, then sat on the sofa arm. "I suppose he told you I'm leaving."

"He told me."

"Theo wants me to go. She thinks it's what I want. I don't know what I want, but I figure it can't hurt."

I looked at Joel as she said that. I said, "You're doing the right thing for sure, Clare."

She looked at Joel and jerked her thumb at me. "What's his problem? He got a problem?"

"Henry's tired," Joel said. "He's fed up and he's not going to take it anymore."

Clare ignored him. "Will you talk to Theo? She was surprised when Rachel told us you'd actually gone for the interview this time. She told me you'd make a great teacher."

I said, "When are you going? I want to talk to you before you get away."

Joel looked back and forth at the two of us. "I have to get out of this shirt. Maybe I'll go over to the apartment and change. I'll be by the pool, Clare, when you're ready."

"This won't take long," she said.

I went to the door with Joel. As he went out he made a peculiar gesture—twisting his face up and raising his eyebrows—that I took to mean find out what I could. I nodded at him and said, "Gotcha."

When I closed the door after him Clare said, "I don't need a lecture, Henry."

"Tell me about Theo," I said.

"She's staying put. She's probably ready, but I'd wait a bit. Can you wait?"

"Sure." I looked around the room. "This is swell. Anyway, I meet new women every day."

"I hear you're meeting a lot of women. Kelsey. Mariana's sister. You've been busy these last few weeks." She grinned. "For an old guy, I mean."

"One doesn't smell right and the other left me a note saying she was pleased to meet me. Kelsey is Rachel's friend. There's no career for me in this business."

"I could have told you that. You're the home-and-hearth type. Solid citizen, that kind of thing. Theo and I talked about it."

"I move back in and nothing has happened—you figure that's how it goes?"

"Maybe so, maybe not. I mean, I could be wrong. Theo surprises me—this thing between us surprised me."

"You told me," I said.

"She got something she wasn't getting." Clare held up her hand. "No jokes, please."

I shook my head.

"Rachel wants you back in the worst way. She really loves you."

I looked at my feet. I was very tired. I could feel it in my shoulders and at the back of my neck. "So what about Joel?" I finally said.

"He gets to hold the bag. I'm sorry about it, but I've got to think of me too. I want to go to Colorado."

"Jeweler to the stars," I said.

"I thought we were playing fair, Henry. I know he's a jerk. But I like him well enough. Joel knew that all along. He knew that going in."

"That's like not knowing it," I said.

"Hey—this is a human body, remember?" She ran her hands up and down in front of her. "It's getting old and stuff." She got up and marched around the room touching things—the lamp, the light switch, the ratty curtains Nassar had promised to replace. "I just want to get out of here and Joel can't help. I can't help him, he can't help me."

"We're not talking about help, are we?" I sat down again. "I mean, maybe we are. I thought we were talking about muddling along. You know, handling the shit."

"O.K. So you got me. He's a dead man, a croaker. A slow guy on the paddle. Not what I want. I figured it out. That happens sometimes, you figure things out. Maybe you don't, but I do. So, I'm taking off. He's mean and ugly and he screws like a bird—what do you want me to say? I thought maybe I could rearrange his face, fix him up, but nothing doing. He's got ideas."

"So does Wayne Newton," I said.

"Not fair," she said, stopping behind the couch. "I wish you'd stop calling him that. Ten years ago he made him some stuff and I was impressed. So what? It's not like that now. It's some other way. I'll have a garden, go to the store—" She stopped midsentence and turned toward the dining alcove, her arms outstretched statue-style. "Jesus. Am I a sucker or what?" She picked up her purse, came across the room, stuck her hand out. "I'm going," she said.

"I know," I said, taking her hand. Her fingers were dry and stubby. I'd never thought about her fingers.

I GOT UNDRESSED and into bed when Clare left. One of the music video shows was on television, so I watched that for about an hour, propped up on the pillows, watching the reflections of Nassar's courtyard lights on the ceiling of my apartment when there weren't any pretty women on the screen. I got up once to get a Tab out of the refrigerator and to turn down the thermostat. Kelsey's song was on the program and there were a couple of other songs I recognized. Eventually, I fell asleep. At three I woke up from a dream about a woman I'd known in college, a woman to whom I'd been attracted, but with whom I'd never slept. We were together on an old slatted wooden pier that ran out over the water somewhere along the Gulf of Mexico. It was late afternoon, cool because a thunderstorm was nearby. There was that feeling in the air of the end of summer, the start of fall, that feeling of release and freshness. We were alone except for a few red-faced men in dirty undershirts and too-large work pants who were behind her, off in the middle distance, working on shrimp nets, painting boats. The woman was wearing a light-colored sundress, a dress with a full skirt. She was sitting on an old automobile tire with her knees up and open, the skirt pushed down between her legs. She said, "I want to show you something," and pulled the skirt up, spreading her legs. Her clitoris was two inches long and rectangular, and at its tip there was a point, like an Indian arrowhead. The thing curved upwards like a small, erect penis. She clamped the skirt under her chin and reached between her legs, using both hands to spread her labia, then smiled at me. Without any other movement—her fingers, hips, and legs were all still—the clitoris slowly, almost

187

mechanically, wagged back and forth, pausing at each extreme of its arc. This went on for several minutes. Nothing else in the scene moved. While I stared at the small sexual part, she stared at me, smiling. Finally, she removed her hands, grabbing the skirt without lowering it, the clitoris still moving between her legs. I looked up at her face, which was full of kindness and affection, and she said, holding the skirt so that she was peeking out over the hem stretched between her hands, "I love you enough to show you this, but not enough to let you touch it."

Then I woke up. I sat on the edge of the bed for a while, resting my head in my hands, stretching my neck and back. I kept my eyes closed and pictured the girl in the dream, and her genuine affection, and the grotesque, Gumby-like clitoris.

The television was still on, but the screen was snowy, and static was the only sound coming out. I crossed the room and cut the volume off, then twisted through the channels. A couple of stations had overnight news broadcasts, ESPN was showing an Australian-rules football match, and the tireless people of the Christian Broadcasting Network were still at it. A shy-looking girl with a broad face and freckles came out from behind a curtain and sat on a barstool at the center of a bare stage, her legs crossed. She was wearing a dark, patterned dress with long sleeves and a high neckline, and she held her guitar, loosely balanced, on her thigh. She talked for a few minutes, smiling, looking down at her knee, nervously toying with the guitar's fingerboard. When she started singing I watched her left hand move over the strings. Her nails weren't colored, but they glistened under the lights, her thin fingers turning white as she tightened on chord after chord in short little movements. Everything she did seemed sexy. I watched her, wanted her to flash that plain lovely smile at me. I imagined her in the dream, sitting at the beach, the rough curly hair rippled by Gulf winds, the dress lifted, the clear tight skin of her thighs, the smile. I imagined loving her, kissing the skin, kissing between her legs—her clitoris wasn't the huge thing I'd dreamed, but something tiny and delicate and wet, the size of a child's nipple, sweet to the taste. I imagined lingering there as she wrapped the skirt over the back of my head, tugging gently.

Then her song was over and the announcer—not the Robertson guy or his black sidekick, but some other guy I'd seen before—came into the picture and started talking to her, pointing to the guitar and then off somewhere behind them. I snapped off the television.

———— • ————

ON MONDAY, the TV woman Jerry Kluge had been so interested in had a whole new setup: new music, new desk, new backdrop. She even had a new hairstyle. She opened her program with some before and after shots of the *NewsNight 14* set, then swung into a detailed tour of the color weather radar with a weatherman she called Wolf. I was going to call Jerry to be sure he was watching, but I didn't want to call Theo to get his number, so I didn't. The woman didn't look like a lesbian to me.

Tuesday, Harold got hit by a car. Rachel called the office and caught me in the middle of an argument with the creative director about a slogan for a start-up fast-food operation the agency had a piece of. I apologized and left the office in a hurry.

Wenzel's receptionist was also his assistant, a young woman with a pretty face and an uncooperative body. Harold was in shock, she told me, as she led me through a mini-labyrinth of corridors and examination rooms. Harold was on his side on a silver table in the last room. One of his back legs was sticking straight up in the air. Underneath him there was a towel I recognized.

Theo was standing at the end of the table with her arms wrapped around Rachel's shoulders and neck. Wenzel was leaning against a cabinet off to one side, flipping through what looked to be a reference book. He glanced up and nodded as I entered the room.

"I have to get Mildred Ransom's bird," the receptionist said to Wenzel. "I'll be back."

I stroked Harold's head. He rolled his eye up to take a

look at me, then gave out a snort and blinked a couple of times.

"It's not as bad as we thought," Rachel said.

Theo pointed to the towel. "There may be internal bleeding. Not this. This is from the leg and a cut over here on his side. That's no problem. The leg can be fixed."

"Will be," Wenzel said. He closed his book and squatted alongside the table, using a pen-size flashlight and a plastic stick to look at Harold's nose.

Harold sneezed, then lifted his head and looked toward Theo and Rachel, then toward me, moving his ears around.

Wenzel grabbed the dog's nose handshake-style and flashed the light in his eyes. Harold tried to jerk himself free, then started whining when he couldn't.

"Slow down," Wenzel said to the dog.

The receptionist popped in with a syringe that she gave to Wenzel, then left again. He squeezed the pump end and asked me to hold Harold while he put the needle into the back leg.

There was some barking from outside, and the sound of the back door opening and closing, then the receptionist came to the examining-room door with a parrot on her hand. "Would you like to come with us?" she asked, motioning with her free hand. Theo and Rachel filed out. I stopped at the door and looked at Wenzel, wondering if I ought to stay.

He said, "I'll just snap it back in place. Won't take a minute."

The parrot sang like an opera star all the way to the waiting area. The room was paneled in chocolate-colored wood, the chairs covered in orange vinyl. There were coffee tables that looked like big guitar picks on legs along the walls. I pulled a *Dog World* with a torn cover out of the stack of magazines on the table nearest me and started thumbing through.

The receptionist gave the parrot to a short woman who

had a wart the size of a gumdrop over one of her eyes. The woman took the bird and inspected it carefully, picking at its wings, checking the tail feathers and the beak. The receptionist patiently waited for the inspection to end, then opened the door.

"Don't worry about your dog," the receptionist said to us when the woman was gone. "We do these car accidents all the time. Everything from hamsters to cows. They always break legs. I don't know why."

She left us alone in the waiting room. In a minute I realized Rachel was staring at me. I looked up and she wiggled her eyes toward Theo. Then she said, "I'm going to take a walk. There's this software store I want to see."

"What store?" Theo said.

"Harold's fine, Mom," Rachel said, patting Theo's shoulder. "Don't worry. I'll be right back." She gave me some more business with the eyes and then left, stopping in the door to point at Theo, in case I hadn't gotten the message.

"Harold's fine," Theo said. "What kind of child is that?"

I smiled and tossed *Dog World* back onto the table. "Good one," I said. "You getting her the computer?"

"I have to, I guess. She doesn't talk about it like she used to. She's not there much, though."

I was playing with the alligator-green ashtray on the coffee table.

"Clare's leaving, I guess you know."

"I talked to her Sunday," I said. "I'm sorry."

"I told her to go. You should see the phone bill—she spends all the time on the phone to Colorado. I don't know how she can stand that guy. I met him when we were out there. He's like a ferret or something. His shirt's always tucked in too tight. I didn't like him."

"Sounds like he's matured."

"He's like some kind of fastidious little short-fur thing. He's got rules, boy, he's got it all figured out. I despise people like that." She opened her purse and brought out a

roll of breath mints. "Want one?" She offered the roll to
me.

I took a mint.

"She's no dream, either. Once you get to know her."

"Joel's upset. He was there Sunday. I think he thought
they were going to stay together. She doesn't like him much.
She told me. In detail."

Theo frowned. "I'll bet. Told you how lousy he is in
bed. She told me a hundred times. I don't know what she
wants. Some kind of TV show or something. She's the pits."
Theo glanced at me. "Sorry. I always forget she was your
wife. She doesn't seem like anybody you'd be interested in.
She's on the mean side for you."

"Tough guy," I said, poking myself in the chest. "Or
something."

"Yeah. You can take a hit." Theo picked up the dog
magazine and leafed through it. "So what am I going to do
now? Maybe I should get Harold a friend. What about that?
Maybe you want to come back?" She rattled the magazine
and looked at the ceiling. "I didn't mean that the way it
sounded, like you would be Harold's friend. Oh, forget it."

"I thought about calling," I said. "Sometimes I wanted
to."

"Sure," she said. "I need to, you know, find myself." She
laughed. I laughed too. "I'm not having fun, Henry. Rachel
says I'm silly. She says we're made for each other." She
shook her head. "I don't know. Maybe she's right. I mean,
you seem O.K."

"I feel swell," I said.

She looked at me, then got up and went across to the
door of the office and put her forehead against the glass. "I
wonder where she went? She could be anywhere out here."

That night I went to Rollaway Lanes and bowled for two
hours. I hadn't been inside a bowling alley in ten years.

The place was full of swarthy housewives and guys in shiny shirts. They looked like freaks to me. I was using a red ball on lane forty-six, the last lane in the place.

For the first few frames I just played around, but then in the third I threw a strike, so I started trying. I made one fifty through nine and then started over when I rolled a strike in the tenth, counting it as the first frame of the next game. I took it slow. I drank a Pepsi that I got out of a machine next to the ladies' room, and I bowled the second and third games as well as I could—one sixty-nine and one eighty. The fourth game I was tired and my arm hurt and I stopped after six frames, all open.

A guy in a hot-pink shirt with MOZAMBIQUE embroidered across its back came up to me as I was taking off my rented shoes. He asked me if I wanted to sub for one of his team members who hadn't showed up. I told him I was all bowled out, which he thought was very funny.

"Come on, Jack," he said. "Give a fella a hand here. We're over on nineteen and we need you." He was about forty, and he had a modern-look crew cut.

I shook my head. "Sorry. I can't handle it."

"It's no big thing," the guy said. "You just get up and toss it down there. It don't make no difference where it goes. We got a handicap covers the limitations of our athletes. I mean, hey, we got a guy with one shoulder on the team. We got a kid makes wind chimes. What do they do? They go a hundred ten, hundred twenty-five. Look at these scores here"—he picked up my scoring sheet, tearing it out from under the metal clip—"I mean, in this bunch you're the heavy hitter. You're the long ball man. What do you say?"

"I say thanks very much for the invitation."

"We buy the beer," he said.

He spread his arms out as if to say that this was his final offer. I looked at the circles in his armpits. "Maybe next week," I said. I took the sheet from him, hooked two fingers in the backs of my bowling shoes, and started for the desk.

"You're a treat," the guy said as I passed him.

I got home at ten and turned on the late news. Somebody I knew in high school called long distance to ask me to come to our twenty-year reunion. At first I didn't know who he was. He said his name and I didn't recognize it. Then, when I remembered him, I was very friendly. I wanted to talk, to find out about other people from the class, but he wanted to firm up his list. I said I didn't think I could come. He said that I was only going to have one twentieth high school reunion and that everybody was going to be there. "Let me put you down for a maybe," he said.

I said that would be fine.

My back hurt. I turned off the television, got undressed, and went into the bathroom. I shaved and took a shower, then straightened the bathroom closet, threw away an old toothpaste tube, a plastic bottle of suntan lotion, and some old pills. I wasn't ready to sleep, so I cleaned up the apartment. I did the whole place, one end to the other, with the electric broom. Then I Windexed the glass sliding doors in the living room. I stripped the bed, swapped the mattress end-for-end, and changed the sheets. By then I was covered with sweat, so I sat down on the carpet next to the bed and looked at my blue gourami. When I was a kid I had a gourami with an eye disease. The eye swelled up into a bubble the size of a marble. It looked horrible. I found out what it was and got the stuff to treat it, but the disease was too far along. It didn't get better. The worst part was looking at this fish all the time. With one regular eye and this other thing, glassy and transparent, ballooned up on its head. The fish floated sideways most of the time, this eye up toward the top—it must have been filled with air or something, because it really interfered with his swimming.

J OEL KNOCKED on the door at eight in the morning. His hair wasn't straight and he was carrying my newspaper and a package of Rainbo cinnamon rolls. "Your favorites," he said, shaking the package of rolls. "Let's have some coffee."

I let him in and pointed toward the kitchen. "You make it. I'll get dressed." I went into the bedroom and put on my pants.

He yelled at me from the kitchen. "I feel a lot better. Clare's gone. Left last night. I drove her to the airport. Big scene in the snack bar out there."

"Oh yeah?" I brought the gourami out of the bedroom, then sat down at the table and watched him wait on the water. "What happened?"

He took a folded piece of paper out of his shirt pocket. "She wrote me a note, can you believe that? She gave it to me and told me not to read it until her plane left."

"So you read it right away."

He was embarrassed. "You think that's terrible?"

I rubbed sleep out of my eyes and then got up from the table and closed the curtains in the kitchen and in the living and dining rooms, then turned on a couple of lamps.

"I wanted to know what it said," he said, tapping on the orange-juice bottle that had the fish in it. "You're killing this guy, you know that? He can't get enough air in here."

"He was supposed to bring a fishbowl," I said. "Nassar. I don't know what happened." I stood in front of Joel with my hand out. "Let's see the note."

"Personal. Highly personal and sexy. Can't show it to anybody."

196

I went back to the table. "Included photographs, I hope. It's always good to get those photographs."

He brought the coffeepot and the cups to the table. "That's a disgusting thing to say, Henry. It's not like you."

"I went bowling yesterday. I'm starting a new life. Does she say anything about Harold in the note?"

"Who's Harold?"

"The dog. Remember the dog? He got hit by a car yesterday. He's fine now."

He got down close to the coffeepot. "The note says she likes me. Actually, it says she loves me. And some things she doesn't like about me." He watched the coffee drip into the bottom of the pot. "I thought it was touching. I mean, I thought it was stupid too, but mostly touching. I don't think a woman's given me a note since high school."

"What doesn't she like?"

He waved the question away. "The usual stuff. I'm not somebody else. I'm a jerk. That kind of thing."

"That'd make me feel good, all right," I said.

"You can't worry about it. The base is there, that's what counts. I'm not in a hurry. She also said that she wasn't in love with this other guy. It's something else. That's why I'm here."

I pointed at the coffee. He poured a cup for me, then snapped his fingers and rushed into the kitchen. "Where's the butter?" he said.

When the cinnamon rolls were on the table he poured his coffee and said, "I've got to figure how to play it."

"Sounds to me as if you're doing O.K. Pass the butter. The last thing you need is advice from me."

"I thought that. But I want to know what she said to you the other night. Maybe there's a clue or something."

"I got the impression flexibility was an issue."

"What about sex?"

I sighed. "Always a problem. You've absolutely got the wrong man on that. More is better, but quality's more important than quantity."

"She say that?"

I looked at him. "Something like that. I guess. I was thinking about Theo, so I didn't pay attention."

"Oh, great," he said. He took his coffee to the window and used it to split the curtains. "She told me that, too. More or less. They all tell me that. I said I was doing the best I could and she kind of looked at me, real steady, you know what I mean? I figured it was a problem."

"Movies have hurt them more than us," I said.

"I guess they want you to fake it. I guess I could do that. What else?"

I shook my head. "Nothing. She's peculiar. I mean, this guy isn't a great man. Or he wasn't."

"That's what Theo said. She said he was a moron. She said that when they went to Colorado she was real surprised."

"I know," I said.

"That's why they came back," he said. "Because she despised him. That's what she said, anyway."

I took my coffee into the living room and stretched out on the couch. The first few seconds were really splendid. He came in and took the brown chair. "In the meantime, there are other people. I've been looking at Mariana. She's by the pool sometimes. She's a killer. All that hair and that hard look of hers. I hear they've got some kind of deal so she can do whatever she wants. Maybe I'll check her out. Or some young girl. I've never had a woman younger than me. Actually, this whole thing, I mean with Clare leaving, opens things up. I may try some stuff." He stared at the wall behind me. "I feel O.K. I really do. I don't think this is such a bad thing. And, listen, I'm sorry about the other night. I was a mess."

"You were fine," I said.

"I didn't know what was going on. Sometimes I need help."

It was hot in the apartment. When Joel left I pushed the

thermostat down to seventy, then sat at the dining table and ate two more rolls.

Mariana called and asked what I was doing about the job. I told her I was still thinking. "Careful," she said.

"I've been worrying."

"Good. But don't be sitting over there with the curtains closed all the time. It's bad for you. First thing you know you'll be dead in the tub or something."

"It's the morning light," I said.

"We know. We've been watching. We see what goes on."

"Joel came over and told me how much better he felt," I said. "Then he said I needed a new tank for my gourami."

"I can handle your gourami."

"Thanks, Mariana." I took the telephone to the front window and opened the curtains. "What time is it? Never mind. I don't want to know."

"O.K.," she said. "I understand now. I get the picture. You figure I'm not helping. I arrange a high-paying job in the breakaway world of higher education, and this is what I get in return. Well, everything's perfectly clear now."

"I think I'm in a bad mood," I said. "Sorry."

"I fix things up for you with my sister Winifred, whom you have previously and wantonly violated, and this is what I get."

"Stop, please. Let me call you later."

"I introduce you to my own personal charms, and this is my reward."

She hung up. Minutes later the phone was ringing again. I didn't answer. I stood there and looked at it until it quit. Sixteen rings. When it stopped I expected it to start again, but it didn't. I went to the window to see if Mariana was coming. She wasn't. It was so bright outside that the pool wasn't even blue. It was some kind of silver color. I went into the bedroom. My stomach felt sick. I got into bed, on

my side, with my knees up and my arms around a pillow.
I wanted to sleep. After a while I went into the bathroom
and took a couple of long drinks out of the Pepto-Bismol
bottle, then ran water for a bath. The phone rang again.
Three rings this time. I didn't answer, but when it stopped
I went into the living room and got the phone and brought
it into the bathroom. I hooked the telephone cord around
the cold-water handle on the lavatory and put the phone
on the corner of the bath mat. I flossed my teeth, then tried
to look at my tonsils in the mirror. It was hard to get my
head in the right position for both the light and the mirror.
I listened to the water run and clipped my fingernails, aim-
ing the clippings into the waste can that I'd pulled out from
under the sink. I missed with most of them. My toes looked
all right. The tub was full, so I turned off the water, then
went out to the kitchen and got a fresh can of Tab, and,
coming back, pushed the air-conditioning control to the
fan setting. The fan made a nice, steady hum. I got a copy
of *Creative Computing* that Rachel had brought and returned to the bathroom, closing the toilet seat to make a
table for the magazine and the drink. I climbed into the
tub and got comfortable, then thought it would be nice to
have the television where I could see it, so I got out, did a
quick rubdown with a fresh towel, and got the TV from the
bedroom. I brought it in, then didn't want it there with all
the water, so I put it on a chair outside the bathroom door
in the hall. I turned on the set but left the sound off,
switched to CNN, and got back into the tub. I folded a
towel to use as a bolster behind my neck.

The next time the phone rang I thought it was some kind
of strange alarm in my dream. I splashed water all over the
place when I figured out it was the telephone and answered
it. My fingers were wrinkled and white.

Mariana said, "My husband wants you to come to dinner."

"Hi," I said. "What time is it?"

"Are you in the bathtub or something?"

"I was asleep." I sat up in the tub, reaching to pull a towel off the shower door. "Jesus. I could have drowned in here."

"We're meeting in the courtyard at five-thirty. That O.K.?"

I asked her to hold on, got out of the tub, dried myself, sat down on the bath mat with my back against the wall and the towel over my head. "O.K.," I said, picking up the phone.

Nassar was on the line. "That you? Boy, have I got a surprise for you." He waited for me to say something, but I didn't. He said, "You there? Hey. Get in the swing of things here. What's with you, anyway? I've got a big thing planned. I've been working on this for weeks."

"Working on what?"

"I'm not telling you or you won't come," he said. "You'll find out tonight. Five-thirty. So long."

He hung up. I dropped my hand over the side of the tub. The water was cold. There was a war on the television. I didn't know which one it was. I didn't want to get up. I was comfortable. I liked the bathroom. It was nice on the floor. In movies, crazy people always sit on the floor. I played like a crazy person for a minute, nodding my head and making a peculiar sound.

T HE PARTY was a barbecue, with guests. Joel was there
with somebody I'd never seen before, a lean and
dark woman who had a sharp nose and wet curly hair. She
was pretty in a beat-up way. Winnie brought a big guy who
said he'd been drafted by the Redskins in the fifth round
two years before, had broken his back in rookie camp, and
now worked for Rawlings. Nassar was smoking up the place
with a homemade barbecue kettle and giving everybody
orders. About six o'clock, Rachel and Kelsey showed up
with Duncan Brown. Mariana wasn't there.

"All your friends," Nassar shouted at me when I went
over to his side of the pool to see how the cooking was
going.

Joel followed me over. "This is really for me, because
Clare left and everything. Right, Dew?"

Nassar swung the big cooking fork at him.

I put an arm over his shoulder. "You're already in cir-
culation. The party can't be for you. Sorry." I squeezed his
shoulder and glanced at the woman he'd brought. She was
alone next to the pyramid doghouse.

Joel grinned. "Naw," he said. "Just met her. Dew set me
up."

Winnie and her football player were bent over the front
of Nassar's cow, staring into the new green eyes. She waved
a piece of pita bread at me. "Come over here. I want to
show you something." She was wearing a peculiar outfit—
giant blue shorts and a sweatshirt with an extra collar that
was sewn on crooked. I marched Joel in her direction. She
switched sandwich hands and stretched her right out to meet
Joel. "You another of his pals?"

"I'm a lonely guy right now," Joel said. "What about you?"

"I'm a hot ticket. Not as hot as your friend, of course." Winnie laughed and did a shallow curtsy.

"He played for the Redskins," I said, tapping the big guy's arm. "Cameron, this is Joel."

"Pleased to meet you," Cameron said.

"I got your message," Winnie said to me. "On the phone. That was funny. I'm sorry about cutting out on you that way."

I studied Cameron for a second, looked him up and down, then said, "I don't know what she's talking about, Cameron."

He grinned and grabbed my shoulder. His hand was huge. "That's funny, Henry," he said. "I met your daughter. She's cute. She's real cute."

Winnie slapped his back. "Cameron," she said. "Behave."

He let go of my shoulder and smiled again, although it didn't seem like a very sincere smile.

The sun was gone by seven. Nassar's courtyard lights sparkled nervously in the pool and on the apartments. New people kept showing up, most of them people I didn't know. Mariana arrived with Jack Stibert a little after seven. She said hello to me and then dragged him off to her apartment. He waved at me and said, "Good to see you again. We'll talk later."

Duncan Brown decided to go home and get Cindy. "She said she didn't want to come, but I'll bet she regrets it now," he said. Rachel asked him to stop at the house and see if Theo wanted to come. "That's a great idea," he said.

Nassar switched from Arabian folk music to rock and roll and turned up the sound system. "This girl has a silver face," he shouted at me coming out of his apartment. "Listen."

Kelsey instantly recognized the new music and tried to get me to dance with her, jumping up and down in my face, but I declined, so she settled for Joel, who described himself as a dancing fool. He left his guest with a couple who apparently lived in one of the corner apartments on the far side of the courtyard. I hadn't met these people, so I introduced myself. The guy's name was Rod, and his wife was Louise. Joel's friend was Ardith. It wasn't until she said she was a friend of Winnie's that I remembered who she was—the woman Winnie had accused Nassar of coveting at the Ramada Inn. She was about thirty, with angular features and skin traced with acne.

"I do production at KPOU," she said, when I asked if she was still at the motel. "Clipboard and stopwatch stuff."

"Good, solid fundamentals," Rod said. "That's the way to go." Ardith gave him a deadly glance, but he didn't notice. "You get them down and you can shoot up like a rocket."

"Boy, that's what I want to do," Ardith said. She held her arms very close to her body, elbows at her sides, hands in front, and she seemed uneasy. Her eyes were dark and they were moving all the time, checking to see who was nearby, checking to see where her feet were—that she wasn't too close, or too far away from the rest of us. The nervousness fit her, hiding what I imagined was softness and infinite patience.

The four of us stayed together for a couple of minutes, then Rod and Louise decided they'd have another sandwich. Ardith said, "You're getting a divorce?"

"Not just yet."

"But you're sleeping around to check things out, right? Winnie told me."

I covered my face with my hands, then took them away and said, "That's not exactly correct. I mean—"

"That was a stupid question. I'm sorry." She lowered her head and went into her scared act for a second. "It's not as cold-blooded as that, I know. It happens. You fall into the jaws of sex." She gave me a pretty look that made me think she despised me.

"I'm not doing so well," I said.

"You're doing fine. What do you want to do, nail me right here and now? Maybe in one of these flowerbeds, or behind the beef there?" She was laughing as if she was pleased with herself for finding a way to flirt and make me a jackass at the same time.

I said, "I was admiring you. I like your face."

"Sure. Your buddy loses his sweetheart and who gets called to slop for her? Why, shazam! It's Ardith." She emptied her drink on the grass alongside the walk, then wrapped her arms in front of her and started for the table where the drinks were. She moved stiffly, her shoulders rocking side to side as she walked. Her hair was wet. The colored lights glinted off the curls as she walked away.

"You are really lovely," I said. It sounded odd, coming out of nowhere like that. And it seemed loud, as if everybody would turn around and listen. I took a quick survey. Nobody was paying attention to us. I shook my head and stepped toward Ardith, ready to apologize.

She stopped and faced me. With the lights behind her and the hair dense and wet, she might have been standing in the rain, soaked to the skin. I couldn't see her eyes, but she stood there for a minute, her arms folded over her chest, her feet slightly apart. I didn't move. We were that way for a long time, it seemed like a long time. I heard a lot of party chatter and the sizzle from the barbecue grill. Somebody off to the side was doing something in the pool. I heard the water splashing softly. Then I heard a little laugh from Ardith. That caught me. I wanted to be in love with her. I wanted to hear that laugh repeated like a new song, and to touch my face to her wet hair, to taste it and to taste the fierceness in her lips, and I wanted to feel the weight of her and trace the bones of her back with my fingers, and watch her dress and undress, or do her exercise, or curl up on a couch to read a woman's magazine. I knew none of it would happen.

Joel came up from somewhere. "What is this? Are you

guys playing chicken? Why are you standing here? Ardith?"

"I was on my way for another drink."

"I was watching her," I said, pointing at Ardith.

"I see." He grinned at Ardith, then at me. "You want me to come back later?"

"I'll get you a drink," Ardith said. "Both of you."

"Not for me," I said. "I have to slink away and remember you for a while."

"This is heady material," Joel said. "I thought the attention was supposed to be on me tonight. What happened?"

Ardith took his glass and swiveled around toward the crowd that had gathered at the drinks table. "Nothing," she said, walking away.

Joel turned to me for the explanation. I shrugged. He shrugged back. "I came over to say that Duncan's here with Cindy. She doesn't feel so great. Theo didn't want to come out."

"She likes to stay home at night."

"Lucky for you," he said.

"You're too happy, Joel. You're supposed to be drunk. You've failed to take the responsibilities of a full-blown relationship, failed to move smoothly into adulthood. Instead, you're smiling."

"I feel pretty bad about Clare. I really do." He messed with his hair, pushing it down behind his ears. "I mean, I do. In theory, anyway. We were doing all right."

Across the pool, Cindy was talking to Winnie and Cameron. The three of them were silhouetted against a light stucco wall. Cindy's arm kept reaching out toward Cameron as she talked, but each time it stopped short of touching him.

"I suppose I'm being adolescent," Joel said. "I'm not ready to cross into the next life-stage."

"Which is what?"

He made a diving airplane with his hand, laughed, then slapped me on the back. "Anyway, I told you. It's an interim decision. We're thinking things through. We're hanging tough." He yawned and rubbed his stomach.

"That's better," I said.

"I'm a loudmouth," he said. "I hate it. But don't be lording it over me. If you're not careful I'll take Ardith and go home."

"I would if I were you." I wrapped my arm around him and walked him toward the pavilion, where most of the guests were. "As a matter of fact, if I were a young man of the free persuasion, such as yourself in the present case, I'd be inclined to get my mojo working."

"That good, huh?" He grinned and slicked his hair again. We'd reached the group. He slid off to the left where Ardith was listening to a tall guy wearing plaid pants. I went the other way and found Kelsey and Rachel, and Cindy Brown. They all had chocolate éclairs.

"Hi, Boss," Kelsey said. "You doing all right?"

"Sure," I said. I kissed Cindy's cheek. "How's the patient?"

"Well, I'm doing fine. Nobody cares about my suicide attempt, but other than that I'm swell."

"We're being discreet," Rachel said. "Besides, it was only Valium. Mom takes them all the time."

Kelsey tapped Rachel's forehead. "Settle down, Little One. Truth is not what we're after here, us being discreet and all."

"Oh, great," Rachel said. She turned to me. "Isn't anybody going swimming? The pool is really clean." She took a too-large bite of her éclair and pointed what remained at the pool.

"I am feeling better," Cindy said. "I'm sorry about everything. It's so stupid. Anyway, I hear I missed you at the hospital."

"I came over one night. Nobody was there. You were asleep. I watched you for a little bit and then I left. I was being male and lonely that night. It was O.K."

"I wanted to ask about that." Cindy cupped her hand on Rachel's head and rocked it up and down. "Will you get me another pastry, Rachel? That's nice."

Rachel twisted out from under Cindy's hand and grabbed Kelsey. "C'mon. They're going to try a big powwow."

"Theo's been helping a lot," Cindy said. "Not to mention the kid with the high standards, suicide-wise." When Rachel and Kelsey were out of range, she said, "I want to apologize for the business at the Ramada. I think I was headed out."

"Don't think about it. The chicken was a treat."

"Gee, thanks. You're a pal. You're a pardner. What a thrill for a woman recovering from suicide to meet up with a guy like you. The chicken was all right, and, by the way, you weren't so bad yourself."

"It was a nice thing, sort of—understandable. I didn't worry about it."

"I felt like squat when I left. Like some kind of hot monkey, like one of those with the red asses. I don't go around wagging my butt at guys all the time."

"That's what makes it so pretty," I said.

"Now you're cooking. Just hang on. Come right along that line." She made a rolling motion with her hand.

"Right. I was tormented with lust and affection, in equal measures. You were incredibly seductive, yet there was an innocence about you, a touching delicacy."

"My chicken," she said. "Again." She got up on her tiptoes to survey the crowd, steadying herself with a hand on my shoulder. "Well, where's my new éclair? I mean, since we're food oriented." She pointed toward the diving board. "Let's go over here. I might want to hurl myself in."

"Wait until Rachel gets back, O.K.? She swims."

"So what about you? Now that Clare's gone and everything. What's it been like over here?"

"It's fine. You bump into people. That helps. It's like a permanent business trip. You go out in the town and then there's nobody there, so you come back."

"Sounds like me. I do that all the time."

"Watch the weather channel."

"Yeah. I know. Oh—did you hear that Armstrong's mother died? He's having gay blowouts every night. Lots of dapper fifty-year-olds standing in the yard over there. Am I being a little too happy here?"

"I didn't know he was gay."

"Neither did he. Now he's making up lost time. He's going for two dozen diseases in ten days."

Kelsey came back with Cameron and the éclair, and without Rachel. "She's talking to Duncan. They're going around to look at the drawings on the walls. Duncan says the drawings are copies of these Egyptian paintings that were in some movie. Have you met Cameron?" She gave Cindy the éclair, then rinsed her fingers at the edge of the pool.

"Sure have," Cindy said. They shook hands anyway. "You're a big guy," she said, pretending to struggle with the weight of his hand.

A kid who looked like Lou Reed with a terrible cold came up and put his arm around Kelsey's shoulder. "So, how's my bitch?" he said, pulling her head onto his shoulder.

She yanked away. "I want you to meet some friends," she said. "This is Cindy, Henry—Cameron, Bernard Sandoval."

We said hello. The kid had a lot of mannerisms and tics that reminded me of Johnny Carson. Cameron said, "I haven't met your wife, Henry. Is she around?" He looked around.

"She's working on the ark," I said.

Joel was coming toward us across the garden. He tripped on a duck decoy. He fell on his face. The wine bottle he was carrying rolled down the little hill and splashed into the pool. "Way to rock on, Joel," Cindy said.

He got up slow. "Shit. What am I going to do about that?" He pointed at the bottle, which was floating around under the end of the diving board.

"I'll get it," Cameron said. He went out on the board and got down on his stomach, trying to spear the bottle with his finger.

"Who is this dude?" Bernard said.

The board snapped. It was sudden, not slow, and Cameron and board went in head first. Everybody stopped talking at once. The courtyard was quiet. Even the music was off, although I hadn't noticed that before. Nassar yelled, "Get the man out, for God's sake. Is he all right?" He came across the pool apron quick and stood there gesturing for Cameron to get out on that side.

Cameron came to the surface and rolled Joel's wine bottle onto the concrete. There was applause from the crowd. I clapped along, but hung back when everybody circled around Cameron. Mariana, who had been in the apartment the entire time, came out with a huge beach towel. She got about halfway to where I was and then yelled for me to catch the towel, which she whipped into a ball and threw at me. The towel landed several feet away. I picked it up and tossed it to Cindy, who passed it on.

Mariana said, "Who was it?"

I had already started walking toward her. I turned around and walked backward, looking at the group by the pool. "Winnie's friend. He's fine. How come you're staying inside all night?"

"We're playing with the videotape. Jack needs it at school. We're almost finished."

"So are they." I gestured toward the pool. "Maybe I'd better say something to Stibert?"

"Maybe you'd better say yes, but you don't have to do it tonight. I may come over later. We can talk then."

She stuffed her hands into her pockets, smiled a stay-away smile, then headed back for the apartment. I watched her go, and was still watching when Winnie came up behind me. "Don't worry, she'll help you out if you get in trouble."

"Hi, Winnie," I said. "You O.K.?" She started across the

courtyard toward my apartment, expecting me to follow. "Where're we going? Winnie?"

"I want to sit down for a while. Maybe we can sit on your balcony." She went up the stairs ahead of me and sat on the landing, stretching her legs down the steps. "I like Cameron. I mean, he's O.K. and everything, but he's so big. It's real scary. I saw you going for Ardith."

"I was talking to her."

"They all say that. Then they end up in their cars at four in the morning, watching her house. You didn't get back with your wife yet?"

"You don't belong out here. I knew it when I stayed over. Maybe that's why I split. I couldn't feature us and our cereal, you know what I mean? You're not really unmarried or anything."

"No." The party was spreading out again. Duncan and Cindy were still talking to Cameron at the edge of the pool, but the rest of the people were scattered around, some in the pavilion, others walking around Nassar's courtyard. He'd turned the music on again and Kelsey and Joel were by the broken diving board dancing like finger puppets. I couldn't find Kelsey's friend Bernard. Rachel was by herself in a chair next to the barbecue kettle, which was still smoking.

I said, "My daughter's here. There, by the barbecue."

"I met her. She's a sharpie. I don't think she liked me. The kid with her hates me."

"You're imagining things. I go around with them a lot these days. Eat, stuff like that. Kelsey's at the university."

"The college? Oh, university, I see. But you're going to teach next year at Jack's place, right? Mariana said you were."

"I might. Listen, how come I didn't meet you ten years ago, when Clare and I lived here?"

"I was in Salt Lake. That's where I come from. I was supposed to be here for school, but I screwed it. I may still go, though. Hey—maybe I can take your course? Are you real easy? I mean, as a teacher?"

"As a teacher I'm a pushover. A gut."

"That's great," she said. "Leave it to the students. You're not going to teach them anything being a hard-ass."

"I'll report that," I said.

Winnie went to get another drink and I stayed on my steps watching the guests talk to each other. I had a big idea about parties that I tried to explain to Rachel when she came to sit with me. At first she cocked her head, dog style, and stared out at the courtyard. Then, when I'd finished, she said, "Suspended animation. It used to be on TV a lot. On the cartoons. That's what it's like."

I said, "In suspended animation people aren't moving. Look." I waved at the courtyard. "These people are moving all over the place."

"O.K. Reverse suspended animation. They're only moving around in the yard, anyway. Maybe it isn't. That's what it looks like to me. I wonder what Mom's doing."

"She's probably asleep. You should be asleep, too. Where's Kelsey?"

"She and the creep went out to the car, probably. They do that all the time. Sometimes I stay over at her place watching TV and they go out to the car over there. They're exceedingly discreet."

We watched some people form a line to dance to Caribbean music Nassar had put on. He came across and stood at the bottom of the steps. "This is some guy named Crazy," he said. "It's an EP I got a couple of years ago. After this I'm going with the Four Tops. You should be down here dancing. Bring the kid. You don't want to start her off hanging around in the corners."

I took Rachel's hand and held it up. "I'm teaching her to be old."

"Yeah," Rachel said. "And I'm getting good at it. Take a look at this." She froze for a second, her mouth open and her head lolling to one side, then fell against me as if she were dead.

Nassar shook his head and walked away. When he was gone Rachel groaned and lifted her head off my shoulder. "What happened? Is this another world? No? The same one?" She made a disappointed face. Then she grabbed my hair and said, "Are you taking me home, or do I have to wait for Kelsey?"

I reached up to loosen her grip. "Whichever is your pleasure."

"You," she said.

I let Rachel drive to the house. I sat in the passenger seat and thought of things I could say to Theo if I saw her. Rachel checked off what she was doing as she drove. "Turn signal. Rearview mirror. Stop sign. O.K. Anybody there? No. Hit the gas. O.K. Watch out for this guy in the truck. What a grunge. Should I blow his doors off? No. That would be nondiscreet."

I watched her and occasionally told her to slow down, but that was my only advice.

She got us into the driveway and turned off the car and the lights, then waited for a minute before getting out, her hands still on the wheel. "You need any help?"

"What do you mean?"

"Come in and talk to Mom, O.K.?"

"Let me think about it," I said. "I'll go around the block a couple of times, then maybe I'll come." I slid across the seat and punched her in the side. "Let's go. Move it."

"I don't believe you." She locked her elbows at her sides and held on to the steering wheel so I couldn't push her out of the car. I shoved her. "I'll hit the horn," she said.

"Rachel." I backed away a little and gave her an impatient look.

"O.K. O.K. I'm going. You don't have to come back if

you don't want to. I'm trying to help. You guys don't move very fast." She popped open the door and got out. Then, as I got over behind the wheel, she leaned back into the car and awkwardly hugged me, her forehead against my chin, one arm across my chest, the other around the back of my neck. She was strong. She caught me by surprise, pinning my arms between us. I couldn't return the hug, I could only sit there in the driver's seat like a crash-test dummy. When I tried to free my arms she backed away quick. "See you," she said.

I went through the industrial part of town, past a place that made cement pipe. It was late. The streets were empty. Next to the plant there was a stadium-size field that was full of these sections of pipe about twelve feet in diameter. A high Cyclone fence ran around the field. I stopped in a small, dusty parking lot across the street to look at these pieces of pipe. The field was brightly lighted and the pipes, which were twenty feet long at least, lying on their sides, cast dramatic shadows. After a few minutes, two black guys walked by in front of my car. They were talking and didn't even notice me, but I was scared anyway, so I started the car and edged out of the lot.

I headed for the highway. The road I was on was called Attribute Street. I'd been on it a couple of times. At the intersection of Attribute and the highway there was a stoplight and, to the right, an ugly two-pump gas station that somebody kept open late. That was the only building around. Cars were shooting by at seventy on the highway, which was two lanes each way divided by a line of scrawny sweet-gum trees. I was behind a black van that had a baby painted on each of its back doors. The paintings were crude. I could see the brushstrokes in my headlights. One baby had a distorted arm and a smile that looked more like a grimace, and the second baby's head sat down on its shoulders as if it had no neck. It was a delivery van for a diaper company. The hair on these babies looked like pudding.

The light changed. The van didn't move. I backed up a little, planning to go around, but then the driver opened his door and stepped down, waving to me. I checked to see that my car doors were locked, then rolled down my window, keeping the gear lever in reverse.

"Howdy," the driver said when he got back to my car. He was a thin guy in his thirties, wearing a denim jacket with a corduroy collar, and a much-creased straw cowboy hat. There was a yellow handmade cigarette dangling in the corner of his mouth.

"You got car trouble?"

He turned toward his van. That took a long time. He was feeling in his jacket pockets and he must've stared at the van a full minute. When he turned back to me he plucked the cigarette out of his mouth and played with the end of it. "I guess not," he said. "We're doing fine. He just needs a light." He pointed at the cigarette. "You got a light?"

I reached for the glove-compartment door, opened it, fished around inside until I found a package of matches. I handed it out the window.

"That'll do fine," the guy said. "He's gonna keep 'em, O.K.?" He waved the cigarette at me.

"Hell. Keep 'em," I said. I waved and accidentally hit the window glass.

He cocked his head to one side looking at the matchbook cover. "This sure is pretty, this blue color here." He moved toward the front of the car to get more light.

I pushed the gear lever into drive, but I didn't have the brakes on tight enough, so the car jumped forward.

"Hey," he shouted. "Watch that." He yanked the cigarette out of his mouth, leaving a small bit of paper stuck to his lip. He picked at the paper, trying to get it off. "You in a hurry? You don't want to be jumping around out here in the middle of nowhere."

I leaned toward the window. "Sorry. Slipped."

He had the cigarette and matches in his left hand. He moved toward the car and stuck his right hand in the window. "It's O.K. Gave us a little start there."

I shook his hand, which was hard and smelled like gasoline. "I hit the gearshift," I said. "Sorry."

"That's O.K.," he said. "We don't sweat the small stuff." He tapped my shoulder as he was pulling his hand out of the car, then showed me the cigarette again. "Gracias on the light."

I watched him go back to his van. When he was by the open driver's door he stopped and struck a match, which flamed orange. He bent to light the cigarette and then held up the still-lighted match for me to see. I stuck a hand out and waved it back and forth.

He turned left, running the light. I turned right, dried my hands on my pantlegs, and drove back to Theo's house, smelling gas all the way.

The lights at the house were off. I pulled into the driveway and got out of the car. I pushed myself up on the front fender and sat for a few minutes. It was cool. The neighborhood was quiet. There was a bright window in Armstrong's house, but that was the only one on the block. There was enough light to see. The house next door had a FOR SALE sign in the front yard. Dogs were yapping in the distance and there were smaller sounds—crickets, car tires skimming on concrete, a buzzing I couldn't identify. Somebody rolled by in a low car.

I stretched out on the fender, crossing my feet and leaning against the windshield with my hands linked behind my head. The sky was close, smoke-blue clouds pulling across a lighter, distant gray. I stared at the clouds thinking how much I wanted to wake Theo and bring her out.

"Hello, Henry."

Her voice was quiet, tired. She was somewhere by the house. I sat up and looked, but couldn't find her. "Hi. Where are you?"

She opened the door of the screen porch and came down the steps into the yard. The door clapped back into its frame. I slid off the car and started toward her. She was wearing a long skirt and a wide, light-colored belt, and she swiveled with every step, rotating on the ball of each foot in turn— a lovely walk.

"There you are," I said.

"I've been waiting for you," she said. "Rachel said you were going around the block, but I wasn't so sure." We were a few feet apart in the yard. I could see her face, sharp-featured and gentle, a few freckles, her dark eyes. She looked as if she'd just gotten dressed—boots and makeup, her lips glinting, her hair fresh and brushed. I wanted to lean forward and kiss her, but she didn't move toward me, so I held back and reached to get an imaginary bit of lint off her shoulder. She laughed sweetly and caught my hand in mid-air. "So," she said. "I guess Rachel tells no lies."

About the Author

Frederick Barthelme is the author of the critically acclaimed *Moon Deluxe*. He was born in Texas and lives in Mississippi. He is a frequent contributor to *The New Yorker*.

Affair
Prevention